THE GUARD MURDERS

Earl Rasmussen

Tate Publishing & *Enterprises*

The Guard Murders

Published by Tate Publishing & Enterprises, LLC
127 E. Trade Center Terrace | Mustang, Oklahoma 73064 USA
1.888.361.9473 | www.tatepublishing.com

Tate Publishing is committed to excellence in the publishing industry. The company reflects the philosophy established by the founders, based on Psalm 68:11,
"The Lord gave the word and great was the company of those who published it."

Cover design by Blake Brasor
Interior design by Chelsea Womble

Published in the United States of America

ISBN: 978-1-61739-912-1
1. Fiction, Crime
2. Fiction, War & Military
11.03.03

CHAPTER ONE

Patrolman John Gapinski pulled his patrol car into the parking lot of the strip mall. At 5:00 a.m., there was no need to search for a parking space. Stopping his car in front of the closed drugstore, he stretched as he surveyed the scene. The first rays of dawn came filtering through the pine trees on the east side of the parking area. The air carried a smell of rain, and when one observed the overcast, one knew that the promise of warmth brought by the sun's rays would soon vanish.

John left his car and began to stroll along the walk that extended the length of the mall. Trying each door, he peered through the store windows and, using his flashlight when needed, attempted to make sure that everything was normal. He reached the restaurant at the south end of the block and waved to the owner and cook as they prepared to open. Turning to his left, he preceded toward the pine forest and the pathway that would take him to the apartment complex on the far side of the trees.

"Hi." John's acknowledgment of the newspaper boy always occurred where the path entered a wooden bridge that spanned Minnehaha Creek. Waving at the policeman, the young high school boy sped his ten-speed bike up the slight grade and raced at breakneck speed toward the homes that lined the western edge of the mall.

Reaching the structure, Patrolman Gapinski walked slowly along the rail on the north side and peered into the darkness of the stream. At the east end, something caught his eye. He looked a second time and realized what appeared to be an arm enclosed in bright yellow, draped over a limb of a downed tree. He could barely make out the rest of the figure.

Scrambling down the bank, Gapinski slipped and almost toppled into the fast-moving water. The officer rolled up his pants and, after removing his shoes and socks, entered the stream. Ice-cold chills went up his spine as he moved slowly along the tree toward the floating figure. Grabbing the arm, he tugged at the body, moving it toward the bank. Slowly the weight of the torso as it emerged from the liquid began to strain the forty-year old beat cop.

Panting for breath, John sat on the trunk of the downed tree, trying to decide what he should do next. With the body safe on shore, his first effort should be to contact the precinct and report his finding. He hated to leave the scene for the few minutes it would take to reach the restaurant and return, but there was no alternative. He completed an attempt at drying his feet, put his socks and shoes on, and began the climb to the trail.

John was a foot from the path when he spotted the wallet lying close to the bridge railing. He had missed the brown, leather billfold when he had first seen the body. *Maybe it belongs to that poor soul,* he thought as he marked the spot with his now-wet handkerchief.

In 1967, the Minneapolis police department had its headquarters in old city hall. The fortress-like structure, built before the turn of the century, housed both city and county offices. The building took up an entire city block, with its main entrance facing toward the Mississippi River some five blocks distant. When a person entered the great foyer, they had a choice of turning right for city hall functions or left for county business.

Police cars were continually blocking the eastbound lanes of Third Avenue that lay on the north side of the stone structure. From that side of the building, you entered police headquarters down a flight of stairs to the main floor. This occurred because of the downward slope of the streets on either side of the building. The slope was so steep as to climb an entire story in that one block.

The telephone interrupted the thoughts of Detective Sergeant Brian Donnley as he looked forward to the final day before the start of his three-week vacation. There had been no calls to homicide for almost ninety-six hours. *At this rate,* he thought, *the politicians would probably cut the budget and transfer the entire section to the school patrol.*

"Homicide, Detective Sergeant Donnley," he spoke into the mouthpiece, half expecting a wrong number.

The restaurant at the Bridge Crossing Mall opened its doors ten minutes early that Friday morning to allow the police a place to congregate. Officer Gapinski, seated at the far table with two men dressed in street clothes, looked tired and upset. The taller and younger of these two men went over Gapinski's story once more.

"Gapinski, why did you remove the body from the stream?" the detective asked for the fourth time.

For as many times, Gapinski responded, "Sergeant, I wanted to make sure the body did not come loose and move downstream.

In order to do that, I had to secure it by moving it to shore. You may think that was a mistake. I don't."

Donnley could see that the officer was beginning to get upset. He looked directly at him and asked what would be his final question. "Did you see anything or anybody out of the ordinary during your tour of duty? Take your time on this one."

Gapinski sat for at least three minutes, going over his shift in his mind. The noise from the kitchen began to grate on Donnley as he sat there awaiting the response. The patrolman's eyes were closed and the detective thought for a moment that this uniformed brother had fallen asleep.

"No." He paused now, and his face openly formed a question before he could put it into words. "Maybe…but I'm not sure."

"If you think you saw something, then spell it out for me. I'm the expert; let me decide if it's important." Donnley looked directly at the tired officer.

"Well, Detective, it was about two or three hours before I walked my rounds. I'd say about 2:30." Gapinski paused as he searched his mind for the right words. "I usually swing through the parking lot every hour or so to make sure everything's normal. Sometimes there are a couple of kids making out in a car, and once in a great while there's a few partying in the woods. Last night it was quiet. When I drove through the parking lot, I saw nothing out of the ordinary, but as I pulled on to the street, what looked like a military vehicle drove slowly by. I'd say it was going about ten to fifteen miles an hour. We have a lot of military types at the airport, so at the time, I didn't think it out of the ordinary."

Donnley looked quizzically at the patrolman and waited patiently for him to continue.

"What struck me was the time, because usually you don't see military vehicles at that time of the morning." He sipped his coffee before continuing. "It was a dark blue pickup truck. I didn't catch the number."

Donnley jotted the information down, more as a duty than an expectation. "Is that all, John?"

The patrolman nodded as the detective slipped his notebook into his breast pocket.

Donnley turned left on Minnehaha Parkway when he pulled out of the parking lot. He drove slowly through the neighborhood, glancing both left and right, trying to get a handle on the area that Officer Gapinski protected and watched over. There were three locations that were off-limits to the patrolman: the conglomerations of military installations to the north side of the international airport, the VA hospital grounds, and the United States Bureau of Mines, which lay just to the east of the hospital complex. All of these lay to the south of Gapinki's beat. The military installations were known collectively as Fort Snelling; in practicality, they were part of the international airport. They included the Army, Navy, Air Force, and Marine Reserves, plus the Air National Guard. All had an active military presence with their group of advisors. A dark blue pickup could have come from a dozen or more units.

A strip of exclusive homes stretched along both banks of Minnehaha Creek until the parkway intersected Hiawatha Avenue. From that intersection, one could proceed directly into Minnehaha Park and turn left toward Lake Street, some twenty blocks distant, or right toward Fort Snelling. Another stretch of expensive homes lined the west bank of the Mississippi River as it meandered toward New Orleans, some thirteen hundred miles south. The homes faced a similar grouping of houses on the east side of the river in St. Paul.

The rest of the neighborhood was typical blue-collar and semi-professional. Most of the homes were built just after World

War II or in the late thirties. The main thoroughfares ran north and south with a few primary east-west streets. Near these intermediate arteries a scattering of small apartment buildings would appear, giving the casual traveler a sudden surprise, like coming across a lone pine tree in the midst of the Mojave Desert.

Intermingled with this housing came an occasional grouping of stores built in the 1920s and '30s, usually centered at a main intersection. Once in a great while, a scattering of strip malls built in the late or early sixties would emerge. Bridge Square Mall was of the early sixties variety.

Upon arriving at the intersection of Minnehaha Parkway and Hiawatha Avenue, Donnley turned his city car left and entered a restaurant parking lot. The place was renowned for its superb breakfasts.

CHAPTER TWO

Saturday morning was supposed to be the beginning of his three-week vacation. Donnley appeared at his desk extra early and began sifting through the evidence of his one and only case.

The coroners report made for dull reading with its clinical use of medical terms and its matter-of-fact report on the condition of the cadaver. Simply put, the body was that of a white male between twenty-five and thirty years of age, brown eyes, brown hair, height five feet seven inches, about 150 pounds, no scars or tattoos. The victim was beaten with fists and burned with cigarettes. Donnley guessed that the young man died a slow, agonizing death, the immediate cause of, according to the report, was a severe blow to the head.

Donnley placed the report on his desk and glanced at the brown wallet that Officer Gapinski had marked at the scene. He picked it up and studied it. It was an expensive affair made of calf's skin with a number of pockets. There was no identification, no credit cards, no driver's license, no money. It was as though this beautiful wallet belonged to no one. Donnley began to lay it aside when he felt a slight rise in the otherwise flawless smoothness of the outside skin. In one small pocket, hidden below a larger section, Donnley discovered six business cards.

There were two cards from bars in Minneapolis, one from an attorney in St. Paul, one from a doctor's office in Minneapolis, one from an auto repair business in Fridley, and one from a salesman at Dayton's. The detective slowly spread the cards out on the desk top. As he did so, he slowly studied each one individually as though attempting to find out the character of the victim by the type of business cards he carried.

He guessed that the victim bought his clothes at Dayton's men's shop. He had excellent taste, as the clothes the victim wore and the wallet were all luxurious and did not show wear. The lawyer's reputation as a criminal attorney was superb. He was also high-priced. The doctor's card indicated that the young man also used a pricey general practitioner located in the Medical Arts Building. The Fridley auto repair business specialized in foreign-made sports cars—again, a lavish habit.

The last two cards from the bars represented extreme opposites. The first came from a joint located on lower Hennepin Avenue and considered a homosexual hangout. The second was from a lounge whose clientele were rich, famous, and elitist.

The pictures of the victim would not be ready until Monday morning. The fingerprints were on their way to the FBI for possible identification. Hopefully he would draw a match. The victim's clothes, all expensive, bore no identification marks other than the manufacturer and the retailer, which happened to be Dayton's.

Donnley leaned back in his chair and thought about the case. The man had been beaten and burned as though whoever had done the deed was attempting to get information. The way John Doe died may have been an accident or, what seemed more likely, a pre-meditated murder. The lack of any identification, money, or credit cards and an empty, yet fairly new wallet gave Donnley a sense that this was more than a robbery gone wrong. If the wallet belonged to the victim, he was fairly well off, which was a plus. Sooner or later, someone should call in a missing persons report.

Once the pictures were available, he could visit all six of the businesses and see if he could obtain identification. Brian glanced at his watch. "Oh, my god. I blew it one more time." He reached for the phone and dialed his home number.

"It's about time you called," were the first words from his now-irate wife. "The children are ready, I'm ready, and the bags are all packed. Only the father of my children has gone off to his first love and once more forgotten about his live-in mate."

"I'm sorry, honey. It's just that this case looks a little more complicated than I first thought. I'll be right home to pick everyone up, okay?"

His wife of fourteen years made no response as he hung up the phone. Clearing his desk, he began to think about what he was going to do next. He would get his family settled in at the rented cabin and make a quick trip back to the cities on Monday to continue the casc. Hopefully Helen would understand. She usually calmed down once her mad passed.

The drive to Merrifield, Minnesota, took two hours and thirty minutes to the second. From North Minneapolis to Beckman, the only sounds came from their eight-year-old son with an occasional outburst of outrage from Judy, their thirteen-year-old daughter. Helen's first display of recognition of her husband came as a farmer in a pickup truck ran the stop sign in Beckman, almost causing an accident where the side street intersects State Highway 25.

Although a close call, the near-collision broke the ice and the trip began to develop into an adventure. The next forty minutes sped by for those in the front seat. Those in the back acted as though an eternity would pass before they would be safely away from each other. Their car was halfway through Brainerd when traffic suddenly slowed to a crawl.

An Army National Guard convoy traveling southwest on Highway 371, with its usual military police escort, was creeping slowly through the town. Two olive, drab jeeps blocked the intersection as their occupants held up traffic. Brian peered at the oncoming convoy. He began to think of Gapinsky's claim that a military pickup painted a blue color was in the vicinity of the site where the body was found.

Deeply engrossed in his own thoughts, he did not hear the screams of joy from his son as the parade of military vehicles continued to pass the intersection. Although the number of vehicles in the convoy indicated a company-sized unit, their slow speed created the impression that a whole division was passing.

Brian's thoughts were interrupted when Helen's voice suddenly boomed loud and clear. "Brian, wake up and answer your son."

"I'm sorry, what did you say, son?" Brian turned his head so as to look at the boy.

"What's that blue truck doing in the convoy?" His son was pointing toward the tail of the small parade and a blue semi-trailer truck that was bringing up the rear.

"That's an Air Force semi, son." He was now staring at the cab and trailer as it passed the intersection.

Frank Valencio downshifted his semi as the convoy crawled past the intersection of State Highway 25. He knew the final thirty miles were going to be slower than his normal highway speeds, but by connecting up with this Army convoy, he could pass through Brainerd without having to stop.

The trip to Camp Ripley from Duluth was a surprise sprung on him the day before, when he talked to his C.O. It had taken him two days to pick out and load the items selected by his commander. Usually he drove directly back to Snelling, unloaded the various items in the warehouses, and had the semi back in the motor pool before the weekend.

The trip to Duluth Air Base and its salvage yard was the third trip this month. The voyage itself had been a quickie, coming up late on Wednesday, which forced him to start early on a Thursday morning. Since the unit was deploying to summer field training that Saturday as support for the Army National Guard, it was imperative that he set up his supply room as soon as possible—hence the present situation in which the semi could not be returned to the motor pool until Sunday night or Monday.

Frank's mind began to count the trips he had made over the last six months. *Let's see*, he thought. *There were two trips to Kelly Air Force Base in Texas, three to Chanute in Illinois, one to Selfridge in Michigan, and another to Fort Bragg, North Carolina. That had been some trip.* He remembered meeting some special forces types at the Bragg NCO club and proceeding to the Pope NCO club for a few more drinks. He had been lucky to get up and begin his drive home. *What a hangover!* He'd been driving for the commander over the past six years and would probably still be driving for him for the next six.

He would have to borrow a copy machine at Ripley. He'd make the usual copy of the manifest for the unit's clerk. Why Harry Bascom wanted a copy was anyone's guess, but he'd been making those copies for about a year. Harry had some wide-eyed idea that the equipment was not being properly accounted for. If that were true, the old man would be in a lot of trouble. Yet all the paperwork was proper, the equipment was requisitioned in the normal way, and the commander signed the documents.

Yet, he thought, *it was strange that before the next trip, all the previous equipment would almost entirely disappear from the warehouse.* A couple of times, even the old man moved some of the equipment out to his Wisconsin farm. *Oh well,* he thought. *It's not for us to reason why, but only to do or die.*

The turn into Fort Ripley appeared suddenly and shook Frank out of his thoughts. He always got a kick out of the way the highway swung over the railroad tracks and along the stone fence of the post. There were few permanent buildings at this Army National Guard training center. The enlisted men were quartered in platoon-sized tents or in metal look-alikes. Each unit was assigned to an area that had its own small parade ground between the rows. Washing and toilet facilities could be seen at the end of these small, company-sized villages. A sprinkling of mess halls, serving approximately four companies, were spread out over the entire containment area.

To the left of the main gate lay the base headquarters and the warehouse district plus the base motor pool. It was here that Frank aimed the truck. He looked to make sure the club was open as he drove immediately to the motor pool. A khaki clad figure yelled at him to park his semi in the back row. "See you at the club," Frank yelled as he passed the master sergeant.

CHAPTER THREE

Active duty for most National Guard and Reserve units consists of two weeks' training at a military facility. The training is accomplished in the "hurry up and wait" format made famous by the military of all branches. In the Guard, the unit would convoy to a pre-selected site, set up their camp, and begin the process of training to win a future war. In this year of 1967, the Guard contained an overabundance of college fraternity brothers, sports heroes, and sons of politicians.

Each Guard unit usually has an active-duty enlisted man or officer serving as an advisor and a number of full-time technicians. In the case of the three hundred twenty-seventh Mobile Air Traffic Control Flight, this full-time contingent consisted of nine men and one officer or about twelve percent of the enlisted and thirty-three percent of the officer strength.

T/Sgt. Valencio, a World War II vet, entered the orderly room at 3:00 p.m. on that Saturday afternoon, looking for his friend and fellow technician, Airman First Class Bascom. Instead of Bascom, his eyes fell on Airman Second Class Thomas William Trent. Trent was a college student presently in his first year of law school at the University of Minnesota. He was a favorite of the commanding officer. He came highly recommended for the clerk's job by a National Guard General. The general happened to be the civilian attorney of the C.O. and a law partner of the father of Thomas William Trent.

"Airman." Valencio could not stand Trent. "Where's Bascom?"

Trent glared up from his desk. The smile on his face could not hide the utter dislike that he felt for this uneducated wop.

"Bascom's not here, and I don't know where he is." Trent's smile remained in place.

"Is the C.O. in?" Frank was slowly beginning to lose his composure.

"No, he's still in the cities, and I don't expect him till tomorrow morning." Trent's attention shifted to the ringing of the landline. "Anything else?"

Frank felt the copy of the manifest inside the upper right pocket of his fatigues. Bascom was supposed to be here. It was strange that the clerk would be missing with the unit busy setting up their equipment. "No. I've got to see Bascom." Valencio turned and left the tent-like structure.

The first sergeant spotted Valencio as he exited the orderly room. Yelling his greeting from across the unit open area, he waved at Frank. Frank turned to walk toward the top so that they would meet halfway across the open field.

Thomas J. Mullins's Irish grin opened wide at the sight of his old drinking buddy. "Frank, where the heck have you been?" It was asked in a friendly, half playful manner.

"Didn't the C.O. tell you? I picked up a load in Duluth and the C.O. told me to come by Ripley and see him before returning to the cities." Frank's expression was one of confusion and irritation.

"That's strange; we don't expect him till Sunday." Tom put an arm around the supply sergeant. "You look tired. Why don't you go over and lie down on my cot and get some sack time. In the meantime, I'll try to find out what the C.O. wants you to do."

Frank realized that this was Tom's way of letting him know that he'd had too much to drink. He was tired and the rest would do him good. "Thanks, top; just point me toward your hutch."

Senior Master Sergeant Mullins pointed out his quarters to Frank and finished his tour of the area. The unit's personnel were all present or accounted for except the clerk. No one knew where Bascom was. He had not reported in and the first sergeant had covered for him. If he wasn't here by morning, he would have to report him as absent without leave.

Entering the orderly room, he felt a slight blast from the window air conditioner that was noisily operating in the far corner. It was old and beat up, but the C.O. carried it with him to every deployment and each two-week session. Its output was not the most efficient, so all three desks were arranged in strategic positions to maximize the cooling effect. During VIP visits, this strange set-up created the need for lengthy explanations.

"Has the old man checked in?" The first sergeant's words forced the clerk to look up from his book and respond.

"No," came the short reply.

"When he does, tell him the first sergeant wants to speak to him ASAP." Tom's voice turned suddenly cold while his eyes took on a hard look that he saved for truant young people.

The rain began to fall at 6:00 p.m. *The overcast could not be more than eight hundred feet,* thought the first sergeant as he began his daily walking routine. He turned up the collar of his field jacket and began to move more quickly. His walk took him past the mess hall to the one and only hanger and base operations. From there he would cross the flight line to the camouflaged mobile units sitting in the middle of the field.

CHAPTER FOUR

The deputy sheriff pulled his squad car to the side of the gravel road and came to a halt. Two boys, ages nine and ten, fishing poles dragging behind them, yelled for him to follow them. Obediently, the young officer trotted behind as the two boys bolted toward an unseen lake some 500 yards in the distance. The pathway meandered through the marshy area, maneuvering around low spots in order to keep any interloper dry. The deputy could see only a short distance due to the wild grasses that grew in abundance and threatened to engulf this slightly used trail.

They were about 100 yards short of a lake when the boys stopped and pointed toward a clump of trees that formed a small island in this marshy sea of wet lands. The pathway wound from one high spot to another until it came to this elongated hill of solid earth. The island was high and dry, with a clump of oak and pine trees gathered in the center to form a pleasant oasis. On the far side, about seventy-five yards, one could see the lake and its waves lapping gently against the island shore.

The body lay in the marsh, some ten yards from this high ground. As far as the deputy could tell, the discovery of the body was pure luck. The boys spotted it from a slight knoll at the entrance to the island. That spot was the only place where anyone could see it.

The boys explained that they always went to the island at first light on Saturday and Sunday mornings and fished off a small dock located on the lake side. Around 8:00 a.m. that morning, the boys began to wander home when they stopped to play "king of the mountain" on the knoll. It was then that they spotted the body. They immediately ran to a gas station about one mile away and called the sheriff's office.

The deputy studied the scene and began to jot in his notebook its appearance. The body lay in the marsh with no apparent pathway to it through the grasses. His attempt to reach the corpse was unsuccessful due to the marshy ground that began to suck him down as soon as he got five feet from the shore of the island. How the body remained visible was a mystery for the present. One could guess at however he or she got there. It fell on one of the high spots that punctuated the area and therefore stayed above the muck that surrounded it.

The boys assured the officer that the body had not been there the day before, Saturday, as they had spent all day on the island and had not seen it. This he noted with much skepticism as small boys tended to expand on their tales. Hiking back the way they had come, the deputy looked carefully for any indication of a possible trail leaving the pathway. Seeing none, he jotted the information down and proceeded to call his office for assistance. He noted the time at 11:00 a.m. on Sunday.

The State Criminal Apprehensive Unit received the telephone call at 2:00 p.m. Apparently two boys had spotted a body in an area that was almost inaccessible. Unable to reach the corpse after numerous attempts, the Ramsey County Sheriff's Department called for assistance. What the sheriff asked for was the use of a helicopter with a rescue crew from whatever source.

After a conference with his supervisor, the dispatcher put in a call to the Army National Guard. The State Guard Bureau referred him to the governor's office. The governor's office did not answer. A call to the governor's mansion netted a decidedly cool response. The governor was on a fishing trip and was not to be disturbed. Any request would have to wait till Monday.

The supervisor took the phone and began to explain the problem. He was cut short by an unidentified female. Her response forcefully told him that the governor could not be disturbed under any circumstances, period. With that, the supervisor hung up and swore for all to hear. It was 3:00 p.m., and rain clouds were beginning to gather.

Army National Guard Helicopter 204555, flown by Warrant Officer John Gimp, suddenly appeared from nowhere. The rescue party, now thoroughly wet, peered up through the sheltering pines as the strange-looking craft slowly maneuvered for the landing. A sheriff's deputy, taking a deep breath, ran toward the descending aircraft and waved a greeting to the pilot as he let the craft settle on the beach.

"I hear you need some help!" The yell was barely audible above the now gradually slowing main blades. The voice came from the crew chief as he jumped to the ground and began running toward the oncoming deputy.

"You betcha," came the typical Minnesota reply. Hands grasped firmly as both men measured each other for just a split second. Then, in unison, they turned and ran toward the grove of trees.

At 5:15 p.m., the National Guard helicopter prepared to depart the unauthorized mission complete. The warrant officer, with a glint in his eye, walked slowly along the side of the deputy sheriff and spelled out a problem.

If the deputy would state that the body appeared to move, the unauthorized action by the warrant officer and his crew would have required immediate response to save the life of a citizen. This created a justification for the crew to act. Smiling broadly, the deputy once again grasped a hand, this time with more gusto.

The scene on the road as the 'copter began to lift off gave the impression of a Hollywood movie set. Vehicles of all descriptions lined both sides. Although both ends of a half-mile stretch were blocked, civilian cars somehow managed to appear between the red, yellow, and dark blue of the official emergency units. Near the path to the island, the small landing site where the helicopter had delivered the body was visible. Television cameras on top of a van broadcasted the presence of the press, while the *News At Six* crews were visible attempting to interview every person that came off the now beaten down and soggy pathway.

While his wife was getting things settled at the cabin and the kids were playing a game waiting for the rain to stop so that they could get out on the beach, Brian turned on the little black and white TV set to watch the news.

"A National Guard Helicopter recovered the body of a yet unknown man at South Balsam Lake today." The female anchor smiled at the camera. "*News at Six* learned that the body was discovered this morning by two boys, ages nine and ten." She erased the smile but continued to look pleasant as she glanced down at her notes. "The victim was described by the Ramsey County sheriff's department as being approximately five feet ten inches in height and weighing about 160 pounds, with dark brown hair and a rather ruddy complexion. He was wearing a military field jacket and fatigues." Her smile now returned as she once again peered into the lens of the cameras. "More on this fast-breaking story at 10:00 p.m."

CHAPTER FIVE

Monday morning reflected the inaccuracy of the normal TV forecast. It was still raining in Merrifield, Minnesota.+ The cloud cover blanketed the entire area and the slowly passing cold front kept the temperatures hovering in the forties and fifties. "Cold and damp with no relief in sight" would be the normal expression.

Helen busied herself, preparing breakfast in the small combined kitchen-living area of the rented cabin. The two children were trying to make the best of a bad situation. Judy, closed up in the smaller bedroom, buried her nose in her latest romance novel, while Patrick made more noise than normal with his Tonka truck in the living area.

Brian sat at the kitchen table and worked on his fishing equipment. His thoughts strayed to the unfinished case that lay on his desk at work. Brokowsky would get his first look at it about 8:00 a.m. this same morning. Maybe he would call him at about ten and see if his thinking coincided with his partner's.

"How about a trip to Brainerd?" Although he asked it as a question to Helen, Brian knew she would jump at the chance to visit the small mall on the east end of town, and it would give him a chance to use the pay phone to call his partner.

"Sounds great to me." Helen continued to prepare the omelets for the

family's breakfast. She smiled to herself, knowing that what he really wanted was to call his office in Minneapolis. and find out who Mr. John Doe was.

It was no surprise to Dave Brokowsky when the call came in from Brainerd. His partner of ten years would want a complete update on their latest case. It was uncanny how Brian could guess, almost to the second, when reports or clues would appear.

"Brian, how's the fishing?"

"Up here it's raining, and I haven't gotten near a boat." He paused now, waiting for Dave to brief him in on any follow-up developments.

Dave began with the FBI report. The victim was one Harry Bascom. He is ...or *was* a full-time technician for the Minnesota Air National Guard. He held a secret clearance. That's the reason the FBI has something on him."

"Did they say what unit he belonged to?" Brian began to think about the blue Air Force-type semi his son had pointed out on Saturday.

"No, but I plan on calling the State Guard later today. They should be able to tell me. I checked the telephone books and found a Harry Bascom listed in the St. Paul directory." He paused, waiting for a response from his partner.

"You'll have to coordinate with St. Paul; that will probably take a couple of days."

"We better move slowly on this; it appears that our deceased lived in a very exclusive area." Dave sounded apprehensive.

With that remark, Brian's blood pressure began to rise. It was just like Dave to tread carefully when dealing with a case that could become politically touchy.

"Well, see if you can find out his unit, okay?" Brian's voice had suddenly turned hard.

"Don't get touchy, partner. I only said to move slowly on this one." Dave had caught the change in Brian's voice. "Get a hold of me tomorrow and maybe I'll have more."

Silence on the Minneapolis end of the line signaled to Brian that the phone call was over.

Well, I'll be...he thought as he slowly hung up.

The first sergeant stood in front of the C.O.'s desk and officially reported that two men were not present for duty—Bascom and Valencio. Both were close to each other and both were missing. Calls to their residence got no response, and even a search of their favorite haunts turned up nothing. No one had seen Bascom since Wednesday afternoon, and Valencio disappeared after leaving the Contact Club at Minneapolis on Saturday night.

Major Peter Spaulding looked concerned as he spoke to his first sergeant, yet there was something about his demeanor that reflected the opposite. Bascom checked out on two days of annual leave on Wednesday afternoon that no one would take care of until Thursday and Friday. He could attest to that and therefore, it was not surprising that no one would have seen him for those two days. It was common for Valencio to go on a drunken spree and disappear for two or three days at a time. Why he tolerated that behavior was no one's business but his own.

Sergeant Mullins shook him out of his thoughts by raising his voice to a drill sergeant's decibel. "Sorry, Sergeant, I was just attempting to think of why neither Bascom nor Valencio have reported in." He paused only a moment before charging onward. "Have you checked the bars for Valencio?" He paused again only to add, "He's probably on one of his drinking sprees."

"I don't think so, sir. Valencio's been watching his drinking for about six months, ever since Angel left him." The reference to Valencio's wife brought the major to complete attention. This was the first time that he heard of a separation.

"I didn't know that the Valencios were separated." His eyes flickered in memory of a night some ten years before.

"Yes, sir. They still date and go to Mass together every Sunday. It's just that Angel's staying with their daughter till Frank gets his act together."

"Interesting. Do you think Angel knows where Valencio is?"

"I don't know, but I can call her and check it out." Sergeant Mullins looked at the major for approval.

"Go ahead, and let me know what happens." The major indicated the end of the meeting, picking up the headset of his telephone. " Anything else, Sergeant?" The question signaled an end rather than a continuance.

Angelica Valencio stood peering at the mirror on her dressing table. The image staring back at her belied the forty-two years that her driver's license indicated. A blond-haired and blue-eyed Italian, her body was as firm and as trim as her twenty-year-old daughter's.

The ringing of the telephone suddenly interrupted her thoughts. "Valencios'

"Angel, it's Tom." His voice sounded worried and tired. "Have you seen Frank?"

"Not since a week ago last Sunday. Why?" Angelica always dreaded these inquisitive phone calls, especially from their dear friend Tom Mullins. It meant only one thing. Yet, this would be the first time he fouled up on active duty.

"Frank didn't show up Sunday. In fact, we don't know where he is." Tom paused now to allow himself to clear his throat. "The last time anyone saw him was at the Contact Club on Saturday evening. He left there about 1:00 a.m. on Sunday morning with another N.C.O."

"Tom, don't worry about him. You know how he is when he's been out drinking with one of his buddies." *God, I can't put up with much more of this,* she thought.

"This is different. The NCO he left with was Mike Swanson. He's not known for his drinking, and another NCO claims they were not drunk." Tom paused, not knowing just how much to say to Angel.

"Yes, I know Mike; if he's with him, he should be okay." Angel felt a sudden chill.

Mullins continued, "Well, Mike disappeared at the same time as Bascom did." Tom heard a loud gasp from the other end of the line.

"You okay, Angel?"

"Yes, but the last Sunday I saw him, Frank suggested that something was bothering him. He said that I should open his old trunk if anything happened to him." Tears were beginning to roll down her checks. "I just put it off as one of his feeble attempts to gain some sympathy."

"Do you have the trunk?" Mullins began to sense that Frank's absence was tied to the equally mysterious disappearance of Bascom.

"No, and he didn't tell me where it was." Angel paused now. "Tom, let me know if Frank shows up, and let me think of where he may have hid that trunk."

Tom Mullins simple, "Sure thing," made Angel smile to herself as she lowered the phone piece to its cradle.

Teresa Valencio pulled her car into the driveway of the small, white clapboard house. It was funny how this home of her childhood looked smaller than she remembered it. Her mother, sitting beside her, smiled weakly as they sat there looking for any kind of movement.

"Mom, I wouldn't worry about Dad. I'm sure he's all right." Teresa knew her father was a drunk, yet she worshipped the ground he walked on.

Angel simply smiled in return. In the past six months her husbands' attempt to go dry was admirable. That he would fall off the wagon and maybe go on a bender was also possible. He'd been under a lot of pressure and the driving, while he enjoyed it, was beginning to take its toll physically, if not mentally.

Satisfied that there was no movement, Angel slowly opened the passenger door and emerged from the six-year-old Ford. Slightly behind, Teresa glanced at her watch—10:15 p.m. *We should have gone to the movies like we originally planned,* she thought.

Angel reached the porch and, fumbling for the keys, slowly allowed her eyes to adjust to the inky blackness. The house was dark and the overcast sky covered completely any light that would have beamed upon them from the heavens.

"Mom," Teresa found herself whispering, "are you sure you want to look inside?"

"It's my house, isn't it?" Angel did not wait for an answer. "Besides, Dad would want us to look around and see if everything's okay." With that, she swung the door open and, reaching into the entrance way, switched on the porch and hallway lights.

The sudden brightness blinded them, for a short second, to the complete disarray that greeted them. The house was thoroughly trashed.

After eight in the evening, Mendota Heights emergency calls were answered by the Dakota County sheriff's office. The deputy sheriff who received the call on Monday night was young, inexperienced, and anxious for his shift to end. Pulling into the driveway of the victim, he wondered why anyone would want to break into such a small, insignificant house. *Well,* he thought, *I'll make this short.* He did not want to be late for his hot midnight date.

The devastation struck the deputy as soon as he entered the house. Overturned furniture blocked the normal pathways. Cupboards were swept clean with the contents spread broken across the floor. An overstuffed couch and chair lay overturned, slit with a sharp instrument. Padding was thrown helter skelter around the front room The daughter, a striking beauty, stood to one side of the entrance way shaking uncontrollably. The destruction was complete.

"Ma'am,"—the young man took a tentative step toward the older woman—"may I inspect the premises for my report?"

The blond-haired woman, looking aged beyond her years, simply nodded her head.

The person, or persons, that broke into the home cared nothing for a woman's precious objects or a man's everyday items. The destructive force that struck this simple structure was completely alien to anything that the deputy had studied or heard of. Slowly he meandered through the small five room house. His report began to look like a small book as he attempted to describe each of the rooms. When he completed his tour, he returned to the living room.

The blond, older woman was in exactly the same position as she had been when he left some half an hour before. The daughter, her chestnut brown hair in disarray, sat next to her mother with one arm around her in a protective way.

Glancing at his watch, the deputy realized that his date would be waiting for him in exactly fifteen minutes. His attempt at an interview began to disintegrate into a sort of self-assessment as the young man began to answer more and more of the questions himself. With ten minutes remaining, the deputy finished by adding his own thoughts as though they belonged to the older woman, who had uttered no intelligible words. With a flourish, he shoved the form into the hands of the still-shocked women and pointed to where they were to sign.

With formalities completed, he hurriedly asked if they were all right. When both nodded an affirmative, he said good night and rushed for his car. There were ten minutes remaining on his shift, just enough time to reach the office and check out. *This crime, while depressing,* he thought, *was obviously the work of some punk kids with nothing better to do than thrash other people's homes.*

CHAPTER SIX

The lake began to reflect the rays of the sun before the eastern shore even knew that the day would be warm and cloudy. The tall pines and maples formed an almost perfect screen against the intruding sun for the cabins stretching along that part of the lake. On the western shore, the white bark of the scattered birch gave the early rising viewer the impression that they served as God's special sentinels.

The panoramic view instilled a sense of awe in the old man as he prepared his fishing boat for a day on the waters. His bride remained in bed while the aroma of brewing coffee filled the air. His rising at 4:30 a.m. and fixing the special brew for their breakfast was a ritual that began on their wedding day, some forty years earlier.

Standing on the dock, he had a perfect view of the shoreline stretching both north and south. Once the fishing gear was safely aboard the boat, he would set out along the shore and walk some fifteen minutes to a small marsh that blocked any casual walkers approaching from the north end of the lake. At that point, he would turn and walk the fifteen minutes back to his cabin and greet his wife as she slowly emerged from the bedroom.

The old man always wondered about the cabins on the western side of the lake. There were six in all, covering close to two miles of shoreline. The two in the center, built of whole logs, resembled each other and were extremely large. They were built about five years earlier by, the villagers claimed, a retired general. He could not verify that, nor did he know anyone who could. The builders, acquaintances of his, knew only that their checks came from a corporation.

The strange thing about the entire building project was the electrical system. An eastern outfit installed it and flew their men in and out as the building progressed. Locals claimed that an electrically charged fence protected the whole western side of the lake. The old man thought such talk was crazy.

The remaining four cabins blended with the natural setting of the surrounding area and were much smaller than the two larger buildings. Also built of logs, they matched the larger structures. The general contractor for these four building came from California. The choosing of the contractor over the locals had something to do with national security. From that point on, the locals ignored the area and grew cold to its inhabitants.

The old man reached the swampy area and began the turn for his return trip when a noise caused him to stop cold. The darkness was disappearing more rapidly now, and the old man focused on a dark shape some ten feet from where he was standing. A slight movement caused shivers to radiate down his back. The form appeared to be human. Slowly the form moved in his direction while the voice softly whispered a plea for help.

"Can you walk?" The old man stared in disbelief at the almost unidentifiable man.

"I think my leg is broken." The man began to sob slightly, as any movement caused the pain to become almost unbearable.

"Wait here. I'll fetch my neighbor and be back in about a half hour." The old man turned to leave when he suddenly stopped short. Turning back, he looked once more at the injured man. *What the heck,* he thought, *I'll ask his name later.* With that, he once again turned and began to trot toward his summer home.

Donnley awoke to a morning that was unbelievably beautiful. The crisp morning air gave new meaning to life. He would call his partner in crime and maybe do some fishing. His son, already building roads on the beach with his construction equipment, surely would jump at the chance to catch some pan fish or, if luck would have it, a walleye or northern.

Hurriedly dressing, the vacationing detective quietly stepped out the door and began his morning trek toward the pay phone at the main lodge. The antics of a long-legged sandpiper brought him to a stand still. The bird caught his attention by squawking loudly and struggling mightily with what appeared to be a broken wing. She moved toward the lake, attempting to draw his attention away from a more valuable prize—her nest with its cargo of three eggs. Once she realized that her shell game had not fooled this giant outsider, she streaked back to her home and took up a protective stance, ready to fight to the death for her unborn young.

Donnley's subtle methods, by which an investigation could be misdirected, slowly turned his facial muscles from those of a smile to a frown.

The phone rang eight times before Brokowsky managed to respond with a harsh, half-shouted "Hello."

"Tell me again how you got the information on our victim." The words were clipped and hard while the speaker didn't bother to introduce himself.

"Brian, it's 6:00 a.m." Dave did not like what he heard in the tone of Brian's voice.

"Dave, you said our victim was a homosexual and probably killed by a lover." Brian did not like the idea of grilling his partner. "How did you get that information and from whom?"

"Look, Brian, I can't tell you much because it deals with the military, but there's an ongoing investigation on our victim, and it looks like he was as queer as a three-dollar bill."

"Okay…now who told you, or did you read it?"

"Brian, I'm not at liberty to say, but you know I'm in the Guard and I'm privileged to some information that you're not." Dave stopped now and wondered how far he could go.

"Okay, captain, when are we going to forget the bull and share all the insider information?"

Brian flung the word *captain*, more as an insult than a mark of respect.

"Brian, I will let you know on a need-to-know basis only, and then, only when I'm properly briefed by my superiors." Dave did not like the way the conversation was ending.

Brian slammed the phone down to signal the end of the conversation and his displeasure at being left out of part of the investigation. "Who do the military think they are?"

The Sherburne County sheriff's office responded to a call from an old man on Clear Lake at 6:10 a.m. The deputies, arriving at the residence at 6:25, found him waiting on the gravel road leading down the east side of the lake. By this time, a neighbor was with him, plus the man's wife.

Pointing in the direction of the marsh, the group began hurrying toward the north end of the lake. The deputies drove along the road until it came to a dead end. At this point they joined the group on the beach and began to journey the last two hundred yards on foot. At 6:50 the group arrived at the spot where the old man claimed to have seen the injured man.

"I don't understand!" The site was empty and everyone began to stare at him as though he was senile.

The deputies were the first to question the viability of the old man. The older of the two glanced at the old man with a kind of fatherly look reserved for a truant nine-year-old. The tone of his voice gave the same impression. "Tell us again what you saw!"

Thinking hard, the old man began what had become a repetitive saga. "He was lying right there," he said. Pointing his finger, he indicated a spot some ten feet from their position. "He said he thought his leg was broken and he seemed to be in pain when he attempted to move." The old man paused now and looked at the eyes of the questioning deputy.

"Go on." The deputy's tone was patronizing.

Seeing the look on the deputy's face, the old man simply shrugged his shoulders. *What the hell?* he thought. *No one is going to believe me anyway.* Out loud he heard himself saying, "Maybe my eyes were playing tricks on me, and I only thought I heard him speak."

The older deputy looked at his partner and smiled. "Well, I think we'll just call this a false alarm and get back to our patrol.

Taking the old man's wife by her arm, the deputy slowly moved away from the group and whispered, "I think you should have him checked at the doctor's. It may be nothing, but then again, it could be the start of a serious illness." The wife, on her part, simply stared in disbelief at the deputy and walked back to her husband.

The next-door neighbor wasn't so sure that the old man was becoming senile. He was the first to notice the slight imprint in the high grass that led to the marsh. He was also the first to step into the muck and began to look carefully at the site.

"Did you find anything?" The shout came from the older deputy, and the tone of his voice indicated that he thought this was a wild goose chase.

"No," he lied. *The old man deserved more respect than those two protectors of the law have shown,* he thought, as he bent to inspect a small area and pick up an item that caught his eye.

The deputies looked at each other, smiled, turned away, and began to walk back to their automobile. "We'll fill out the report, and you can sign it, if you'll come with us."

The old man winked at his neighbor. "I'll be back as soon as I get rid of these two," he whispered as he passed his wife.

His wife smiled brightly at her husband and turned to help the neighbor in his careful search of the site.

Donnley got the message just as he docked the fourteen foot Lund fishing boat. His son beamed with pride as he showed off the string of sunfish and jumbo perch that he and his father had caught. Brian smiled as his son related the adventure to his sister and mother. He could not remember his son being happier in the entire eight years of his existence.

The message from his partner simply said to call the office at his discretion. Brian smiled to himself as he realized that the 6:00 a.m. phone call must have shaken something loose. Maybe the military wasn't the arrogant organization he remembered.

Dave Brokowsky answered the call in a voice and tone that was completely changed from early in the morning. His voice was pleasant, yet professional. When he realized that his partner was returning his call, he spoke quietly, as though not wanting to allow anyone else the privilege of hearing him.

"Brian, I'm sorry I didn't let you in on everything I have, but I called my C.O., and he gave me permission to fill you in on our investigation." He stopped to allow Brian to respond. On Brian's end there was nothing but breathing, and the pause became an embarrassing moment.

"I have two things for you," Dave began again, hoping that the information would calm his partner. "First, our victim comes from the 1327th Air Traffic Control Flight, and that unit is up at Ripley for summer camp." Once again he paused before giving Brian the news he prayed for. "You have the general's permission to interview the unit members. They are expecting you this afternoon or tomorrow." Again he paused.

"What's the second thing?" Brian's voice did not reflect any enthusiasm or excitement, but more disbelief. Brian smiled to himself, realizing fully that his partner must be sincerely trying to untie the knots. Yet he did not want Dave to realize he was grateful for the attempt because he wanted to keep the pressure on.

"Once you get through interviewing his unit, you can see all the files on our investigation. How's that, old buddy?"

"Thanks, Dave. I'll start on the interviewing this afternoon and go at it again tomorrow." It was Brian's turn to pause. "Can you set me up with a room at the base?" Brian threw that out just to see the response. If the military was really cooperating, they would find room for him. If not, he could always drive the forty-two miles back to the cabin.

"Sure, if you don't mind sleeping in an aluminum tent." Dave smiled to himself, knowing full well that Brian would get the royal treatment and probably be put up in one of the VIP cabins or, and this was stretching it a bit, maybe even Valhalla—the governor's quarters.

"A pup tent would suit me fine. Who do I see when I arrive?" Brian already planned on seeing the provost marshal on arriving, so it was no surprise when Brokowsky confirmed his plan.

"Okay, I'll leave about 2:00 p.m. and be there about 3:00. Let them know I'm coming and that I need quarters." Brian hung up the phone and began the trek from his cabin. He hoped his wife wouldn't be too upset about him being gone for the night.

Similar to all military posts, the people who choose the unit's site are individuals whose sole purpose in life is to augment each serviceman's time in purgatory with a little practice on earth. Couple the site with the military's choice of middle management, the non-commission officer, and these selection boards succeeded beyond their wildest dreams.

A military installation at three on a summer afternoon can be an oppressive, hot, treeless plain where strangers are a rarity and something to be suspicious about. Fort Ripley did not quite live up to that axiom, as trees sprinkled the plain and offered some shade, at least for the streets. Air conditioning in the post exchange, NCO, or officer's club and in some individual offices offered respite for the few. Most men toiled in the oppressive heat with remarkable, upbeat attitudes, at least in relation to the weather.

Brian arrived at the main gate at exactly three in the afternoon. The heat of the day reached toward ninety degrees with a humidity that hovered in the '70s. A young M.P. gave him a brief once-over before allowing him through the gate. After receiving directions to headquarters, he turned left at the south end of the parade ground and proceeded to a large, brick building that sat facing the road. He parked his car under a tree and sat for a while to collect his thoughts. Three minutes later, swearing from the intense heart, he climbed the steps leading to the base commanders' offices.

Cordial greetings met him as soon as he entered the general's office. The cool breeze from the five-ton window air conditioner felt good after the heat of the parade ground. The general smiled and grasped the detective's hand with his right hand. The warm, strong clasp surprised the detective and gave him a feeling of friendship that he did not expect.

"I understand that you're investigating the death of an enlisted member of the Air National Guard?" The general stated the question more as fact than an inquiry.

"Yes, sir," came Brian's reply, as he instinctively responded in a military fashion.

The general simply nodded and turned to introduce the two other officers who had remained standing at attention during the initial contact.

The provost marshal, a lieutenant colonel, shook his hand with the same strong grip as the general. His reddish brown hair, twinkling blue eyes, and pug nose gave Brian the impression that here was a tough old Irishman who would go to hell and back for the right cause. His firm handshake gave the same impression as his look.

The second officer, a major, smiled weakly as the general introduced him. His ineffective handshake gave one the impression that he would rather not be there. Unlike his two superiors, the ribbons on his chest gave no indication of active service. One immediately assumed that this weak imitation of an officer was a politically connected, college educated staff officer whose sole purpose was to keep everything according to the book.

Brian merely smiled at the base legal officer and reminded himself to be careful around him at all times. *What was that term?* he thought to himself. *Oh, yes—CYA.* His smiled broadened.

Brian liked the first sergeant of the 1327th Traffic Control Flight immediately upon meeting him. His concern for the men and his professional attitude set him apart. The commanding officer of the unit came across as a team player whose fear of rocking the boat overrode any common sense that the man might have had. The unit's clerk gave him the impression that rich, smart college kids had thought of a new way to avoid the draft.

He leaned back in the chair and glanced around at his surroundings. The cabin that the military had assigned to him consisted of a small front room, a kitchenette, a bedroom, and a shower. Though the furnishings were sparse, the bed and the chair he was sitting on were as comfortable as ones would find at home. He picked up his notes and began to study them for the fifth time.

He brought his mind back to the interviews. The three men answered his questions in a different manner, and their prejudices and attitudes were clearly on display for a seasoned investigator.

The commanding offer described his deceased clerk as someone he could not fully trust. Any question whose answer became extended found the officer bringing up the victims supposed sex life as though it were an open fact. Brian did not feel comfortable or reassured by the officers' answers. It was as though the gentlemen, by act of Congress, were attempting to protect something or someone from view.

The young clerk, as parrot of his commanding officer, described the victim as "a fairy." When questioned on how long he knew the deceased, his limited knowledge deflated the accusations instantly. His knowledge went back a whole six months. In the reserves, this meant that the new clerk spent a total of twelve days working with the deceased—not really enough time to form an opinion or to add much to the questioning. Maybe he should try a different approach with this arrogant clerk.

The first sergeant was outgoing, forceful, and assertive. His praise of the victim was 180 degrees from the opinion of the commander. For the first time, Brian began to get a feel for the victim's background. According to the senior NCO, the victim was active in the Knights of Columbus, he was in his church choir, and he dated a twenty-four year old secretary who worked at St.

Paul's First National Bank. He lived alone in an apartment in Fridley. He was an only child who had inherited a fortune from his father but was frugal and did not spend the money foolishly. The NCO gave him the deceased's 201 file and, except for the last few entries, he was a superb airman.

Brian closed his eyes and allowed his body to relax in the overstuffed chair. Slowly, he drifted off to sleep.

CHAPTER SEVEN

Brian suddenly found himself wide awake. He was still sitting in the overstuffed chair. The light on the table burned softly, yet the complete silence gave him a sense of impending danger. He rose, turned off the light, and moved silently toward the window. Standing to one side, he peeked through a crack in the shade. The darkness was overwhelming. The overcast sky blocked out all evidence of the moon and its heavenly partners.

Slowly, Brian eased the window shade upward. With his eyes growing accustomed to the dark, he began to make out the shape of the tree line directly across the street. A distant clap of thunder startled him. Moments later, a bolt of lightening, somewhere to the west and behind him, lit the night. A parked military vehicle became visible in that split second of time.

The gentle knock on the rear door caused him to turn and look toward the small kitchenette and the bedroom beyond it. He waited, trying once again to adjust his eyes, only to have the heavenly laser show light up the darkness once more and spoil the attempt. The second knock became louder, causing Brian to move cautiously toward the rear of his quarters. Slowly he unlocked the door, stepped to one side, and gently pushed the door open.

Senior Master Sergeant Mullins peered into the darkness. "Brian, it's Mullins and a friend."

With that, a bolt of lightening lit up the door frame, and Brian could make out Mullins and a blond woman standing just outside the door. Brian quickly bid the two to enter just as the first raindrops began to descend upon them. Brian closed the door and, reaching for the light switch, felt Mullins's hand gently restrain him.

"Close the bedroom door first. It will keep the front of the cabin dark."

Mullins's statement brought a quizzical look to Brian, but he slowly made his way around the bed and made sure the bedroom door was secure.

"Why did you want me to do that?" Brian's question came out with a slight apprehension showing in his voice.

"That's not my vehicle across the street." Mullins made the statement calmly as he carried a file-sized metal box into the room. Turning to the blond woman, he smiled and held out his hands to take her raincoat.

Brian offered the only chair in the room to this friend of Mullins.

"Brian, this is Angelica Valencio. She's the wife of Frank Valencio, our supply sergeant." Mullins pointed at the file now plopped down in the middle of the bed. "He disappeared some time Sunday morning. That's his file."

"Call me Angel." The soft, feminine voice was barely audible above the rain that was now beating heavily against the cabin roof. "Frank told me that if anything ever happened to him, I was to take his file to Tom."

Brian eyes moved quickly from one to the other of his uninvited guests. *What connection was there between the disappearance and the murder investigation?* he thought to himself. Finally, he allowed his gaze to settle on Mullins and waited for an explanation.

Mullins did not like the job that he was about to do. All his adult life he had served in the Armed Forces of the United States, either with the active or the reserve forces. To now wash out the military's dirty linen in front of an outsider went against everything that he believed.

The murder of the unit's clerk at first seemed as a random thing, but the attacks on the victim's character by the commander and his friends reinforced his belief that something was terribly wrong with the system. The disappearance of his longtime friend and military buddy brought home the fact that someone had to take action. The final nail that drove home his decision to open up this can of worms lay in the metal file sitting like a time bomb in that very room.

"What I'm about to tell you must be kept to yourself." His eyes were looking straight into the detective's eyes without blinking. "Anyone you tell—the provost marshal, the military police, your partner. .anyone—cannot be trusted until they are thoroughly checked out, and then only tell what they need to know."

Mullins reached over and gently took Angelica's hand. "I will complete my tale, and then Angel will fill you in on her end. After that, it's up to you."

Brian began to have second thoughts about this trip to Ripley. He did not realize that he was getting into something mysterious affecting the military. Right then, he could have told the two to leave and take the file with them. That would not help solve his murder investigation. He looked at the first sergeant, nodded in agreement, and silently said a prayer.

Tom took a seat at the side of the bed and began his tale. "Her husband, Frank Valencio, has been missing for approximately five days. About a week before his disappearance, in fact, the Sunday before, he warned me in a roundabout manner, that something might happen to him."

"Did he say why?" Brian broke in to Tom's story trying to speed up the process. He could not see just where this whole thing was leading him. For that matter, he did not know why he was getting involved in a non-case. The superior attitude with which he asked the question tipped the other two participants to the fact that Brian thought they were wasting his time.

"Wait." Angel suddenly stood up in front of the straight-back chair she had been occupying in the corner of the room.

Angel looked directly at Mullins, her eyes searching for guidance. For the first time, Brian realized that there was more between these two than professional courtesy. He did not think it was sex, but something more like a brother-sister relationship. The look in their eyes as they peered at each other gave an outsider the feeling of intruding into a special relationship that had existed for many years.

"Detective, this is a serious situation, and you are not going to understand what you're involved in unless you allow me to tell it like it is." The sergeant's voice suddenly turned cold and military in tone.

Brian smiled and grasped Mullins hand in a firm grasp. His eyes met the eyes of Mullins and held there for a moment. Both men took the measure of the other, and both liked what they saw.

"Okay, sarge, let it rip." Brian dropped his hand, his smile disappearing.

"Sergeant Valencio has been the sole semi-truck driver in the unit for the past eight years." Mullins motioned toward the file. "These files represent about seven of those eight years." He pulled one out and gave it to Brian to look at. "You will note they consist of orders and other documents detailing the history of each shipment from the time Frank picked the items up until it somehow moved on. Each folder represents one semi-trailer load of military items released to the MARS program." Mullins stopped for a moment to allow Brian to glance at the folder in his hands. "This AFCS commander has always been the state director of the MARS program and is the contact point for all equipment funneled into that program."

Brian held up his hand. "Before you continue, what is MARS?"

Tom Mullins looked sheepish. "I'm sorry. MARS are initials standing for Military Air Radio Service." He smiled broadly as he continued, "It funnels military gear, free of charge, into the hands of civilian ham radio operators who, in turn, operate a civilian radio net for the military."

"What's wrong with that?" Brian was still not sure of the necessity of going over this problem.

"Nothing. In fact, when run properly, it's a great program." Mullins frowned before plunging on. "A problem creeps in when the program is not used properly and, in fact, creates wealth where there is none."

Brian frowned and began to study the documents in the file. His mind raced forward as he realized that much of the equipment that was ordered did not fit into the ham radio area. There were computers, jeeps, electronic surveillance items, file cabinets, airborne radar, navigational aid equipment, and numerous other miscellaneous items. This one shipment represented a few hundred thousand dollars worth of supposedly excess government items. Brian glanced at the open file case. There were probably fifty such files in that drawer. Hair began to rise on the back of his neck.

Mullins continued, "Our commander has a side business in electronics." The sergeant smiled now and went on, "It is a small corporation with only four stockholders. His clients are a number of major corporations, a university, and a few of the county sheriff's departments. In addition, he has a few rich individual customers from Edina, Minnetonka, and Woodbury. I was inadvertently present when one of the stockholders commented on the nice dividend he received at Christmas. In point of fact, it wasn't a secret, and the commander often took off for a day or two on his corporate business at least twice a month, although I think he never took personal leave. Last year our clerk came to me with a difficult situation. It seems the commander went on active duty for nine months to attend school at Keesler Air Force Base. Every two weeks, he would fly in to Minneapolis on a Friday night, pull duty in the Guard for Saturday and Sunday, and fly back to Keesler on Sunday night." The sergeant paused to wait for a response.

Brian's only comment was "So what?"

"The commander got triple pay for the period of time he was in town, and the Air Force paid for roundtrip tickets on Northwest Airlines each time he came home. In effect, there was a conspiracy to defraud the United States Government." Mullins smiled at Angel and plunged on. "This, coupled with what Frank told me about these shipments, made me realize that it was more than just a few dollars and that more people were involved than the commander."

"That's not enough to kill someone for." Brian was getting frustrated.

"That's true, but when one studies the shipments for the last three years—that is 1965, 1966 and 1967—one finds a recurrent item showing up." Mullins reached over and flipped the stack of papers to one that had a red line under one of the items. "That item represents a fireproof, security-type file cabinet, equipped with lock and bars. To date the MARS program received thirty-seven such files over the past three years."

"Why is that so suspicious?" Brian was still playing the devil's advocate.

"If it had been one or two there would be no question, but when that many show up approximately one month apart over a three-year period, one begins to think it may be a little questionable." Mullins looked at Angel and gave a big smile. "About eight months ago, Frank got suspicious and laid out the problem to me." The first sergeant suddenly stood up and stretched; it was now 0100, and the storm had let up and was now leaving only gently-falling raindrops in its place.

"The files would arrive at the unit warehouse and disappear about one week after the delivery." The rain was beginning to beat harder. "The receipts always listed a member of MARS as receiving the file cabinets."

"That sounds as though a lot of individuals wanted a file safe." Brian's words, spoken more in jest than a serious statement, brought forth a smile from the other two.

"That's what we thought, so our clerk began cross checking the individuals to see if they did indeed have such a file." Sergeant Mullins grimaced slightly. "I think the cross-checking is what got him into trouble. What he found was that no individual on the list, except the first one he called, had such a file."

"Okay. So far we've got some misappropriation of government property, some fraud in relation to government wages, and a supposition that someone killed your clerk, who was connected to these thefts. That's still not enough for me to go on." Brian's interest was up but not to the point that he actively wanted to pursue the lead.

"There is one more item that you should know: There were only twelve total file cabinets being transferred to the MARS program; except for the first file, the other twelve serial numbers matched each other." Brian looked unbelieving at the first sergeant as he continued. "The file cabinets were somehow recycled through the system and used again some three months later."

"What you're saying is that there was a core group of thirteen file cabinets, one of which arrived at a point where it supposedly still is, while the other twelve were used over and over again?"

Brian's mind was beginning to whirl again. It was too early in the morning for this.

"That's right. As far as we can find out, each file cabinet has been used at least six times." He paused now, more for effect than need. "That means that there was a pipeline in and out of the military."

Brian's look was still one of disbelief. "How do you know such a thing occurred?"

"We checked the serial numbers on the files and then we cross-checked to make sure." Tom could see that this latest information was beginning to stir some interest.

"All right. Have you figured out what they, whoever *they* are, were doing as they shuffled file cabinets around?" Brian began to think some bad thoughts as he waited for the first sergeant to speak.

"When Frank told me about his problem, I suggested that we should try to get some evidence on the major and then we could proceed." He looked sideways at Angel, but she was concentrating on a file that she had pulled from the stack. "Frank's response was that the file cabinets were always locked with a padlock on the bar."

"What good is a locked file cabinet to someone who didn't have a combination?" Brian was beginning to think that the whole military was out of its mind.

"Frank figured that one out right away. The padlock was the commander's birth month, day, and year." Angel laughed now for the first time in the last week. Both men looked at her, suddenly realizing that she had been listening without seeming to. "I'm sorry. But Frank took about four hours trying out different combinations before he finally used the right combination." She smiled up at both of them.

Brian responded, "That could be just a coincidence."

"That's what we thought, so we waited for the next shipment about four months ago and sure enough, the combination was the same." Tom was smiling now as he began relaying the rest of the story.

"So we slipped the lock bar out and took a very hard look at that filing cabinet." Angel now took a seat next to Tom and reached out her hand. Tom took it tenderly and paused in his story.

"What did you find?" Brian's adrenaline began to race as he realized that the first sergeant was on to something.

"Nothing other than a number of files indicating that all the cabinets had been used in Vietnam."

"Right about the time we were ready to give up, Frank grabbed a flashlight and began to peer into the now-empty file. Again, there was nothing...except way inside on the back portion of the file there appeared to be four screws holding on a plate. Just then, someone opened the door to the warehouse and I stepped back behind some boxes."

"What happened to Frank?" Brian began to realize that the two people who sat in front were linked even more by the fear of the unknown.

"Well, Frank slipped the file drawer back into the frame and locked the lock bar." Tom's grip on Angel's hand tightened. "He slipped behind the boxes with me and we waited." He glanced at Angel before completing. "There were two men, both in civilian coveralls, neither of whom we recognized. They went directly to the file cabinet, manhandled it onto the dolly, and wheeled it out of the warehouse. I don't think they spotted me, but I don't know about Frank. In any case, they left by the way they came in, and we left by the back door about five minutes later."

You say there was a plate on the inside wall of the file cabinet. How thick are the walls of those cabinets?" Brian's mind was moving into high gear.

"About four inches. I have the same thought." Tom now looked at Angel. "Why don't you tell him what occurred just last week?"

Angel sat quietly, holding Tom's hand, and began to relate, in her soft, feminine voice, what had occurred only about a week ago. "Frank told me about the files just after he and Tom were almost caught in the warehouse. He expected another shipment and said he would inspect the cabinet before he brought them to the base. That way, he could pick the time and place for the inspection."

Brian was enthralled at the calmness this woman showed. Her inner strength belied her dainty figure. *How much we underestimate the women in our life,* he thought, as Angel continued with her part of the story.

"Since we are separated, I didn't hear from him again until he was in Duluth on his last run." She paused now to dab a tear from her eye. "He told me he had picked up the load and a file cabinet was included. He was worried because the major gave him a VOCO to go directly to Camp Ripley. He told me he was going to inspect the file and not to tell Tom what he was going to do. He wanted to keep Tom out of any trouble if anything went wrong." Angel began to sob quietly, her story finished.

"How did Harry Bascom fit into all this?" he spoke directly to Mullins.

"Harry was working closely with Frank; they were compiling the history, and Harry was matching all the shipments. Both had files on the shipments, and they traded information. The theory was that if something happened to one, the other could continue." Tom took a deep breath and shook his head before proceeding. "I was supposed to be kept informed as they went along."

"It's 2:00 a.m. and it's beginning to rain harder. Why don't we bunk down here and move out at first light?" Brian's question sounded more like a statement of fact.

"No. I think we better scoot out the back door and make for my truck; it's parked on the other side of the hill. Besides, I want to get Angel safe into town before daylight." Tom held up Angel's coat as she rose from her seat.

The two left through the entrance they entered while Brian, with gun in hand, peered into the darkness. The two ran into the darkness, disappearing within the first thirty feet.

CHAPTER EIGHT

Brian waited almost thirty minutes before he flipped on the light in the front room. He sat down and began to read the two files that Sergeant Mullins had allowed him to keep. They were the most important, and Mullins had copies of both. The first file contained a report on the findings from Harry Bascom. The report gave a history of each file. It began with the manufacturer of the file cabinets, the location of the depot that originally received it, and the name of the individual who signed for it.

The second file folder contained a list of bases where the file cabinets may have been sent. How Bascom got the information was a mystery, but there it was. The twelve that were being used over and over again originally started their military career with an army reserve intelligence unit. From there, the file cabinets were sent to Southeast Asia and a military storage site in Saigon.

A handwritten note attached to that file folder and signed by someone called "Wolf," indicated there were nine storage warehouse sites in Saigon, one of which did not exist. Knowing the military's method of bartering, the files probably did not stay with the receiving unit too long, especially if that unit needed something of greater value from another unit. They were transferred to a non-existent warehouse within a month of arriving.

Brian sat back in the chair and glanced out the window. The gray dawn was slowly lighting up the landscape. *Five in the morning—almost time to get showered and shave,* he thought, as he peered at the truck parked across from his quarters. Just then a solitary figure approached the passenger side of the pickup, opened the door, and got in. The driver started the engine and began to ease the truck slowly away from the curve.

Brian Donnley went to the bathroom and began his early-morning ritual. He thought back on the sleepless night and wondered about the file cabinets. The theft of government property and payroll fraud was fine in relation to a court martial or a violation of a Federal statute, but unless there was a tie into the murders, he could not get involved in this purely military matter.

He began to wonder about the lonely stakeout that the military provided him during the night. Why two soldiers with their military pickup remained the entire night outside his cabin would be a question that no one would answer. Were they there to prevent his leaving and to follow him if he did, or were they there to keep track of anyone who might visit during the late-night hours? Certainly the provost marshal would have the answers, but Brian doubted if he wanted to ask the question, at least on the military's turf.

The rain had stopped sometime during the wee hours of sunlight, but the cloud cover remained. Opening the front door a crack, he could feel the cool blast of air and wondered about the temperature. He guessed it had dropped about fifteen degrees during the night and it must be in the low forties. Well, he would wear a light jacket.

He removed his.38 from the bottom of his overnight bag and put the file folders in its place. He got dressed and found that his jacket did not properly cover his shoulder holster. Just as well in any case, since he didn't like guns. Instead he opted to put the weapon in the glove compartment of his car. He took a tentative step outside and found the air nippy as the middle of November. If this was summer, winter could be nasty. He started his car and began the short trip to the mess hall to meet Mullins.

Frank Valencio stared at the bare walls of the old 1930's tourist cabin. *At least it's clean,* he thought as he began to stir. The rain subsided slightly, and he could hear the snores of his old World War II buddy as he slept in the overstuffed chair that sat in the corner of the room. The splint on Frank's leg was almost professional, especially the one he fashioned out of branches two days before. He started to get up but decided to stay still and let his old friend sleep. His friend's shotgun lay cradled across his lap. He smiled, thinking that the scene would make a great model for a Rockwell painting. Slowly Frank's eyes closed as he drifted back to sleep.

Mullins sat with a group of airmen at the far side of the company-size mess hall, drinking a cup of coffee, when he spotted the detective standing alone at the entrance of the dining hall. The first sergeant immediately excused himself and moved quickly to the table set up at the entrance of the facility.

"I'll buy," he offered, as the mess checker began to explain to Brian that there was a fee for the breakfast.

"You don't have to do that." The response from the detective did not stop the sergeant from placing the exact amount—thirty-five cents—in front of the mess checker.

Brian looked at the sergeant with a surprised expression at the ridiculously low cost of the meal. "It's based on how much our separate rations would be; in the enlisted case, that is about

$36.00 per month." The sergeant smiled broadly. "Now you're bought and paid for."

"Hey, I may be had, but I'm not cheap." Brian's remark made Tom think of his active duty days and how, on $75.00 per month, a man had to ration himself carefully so he didn't end up in the hands of the payday loan sharks.

"Over there." Tom pointed to a table that sat at the far corner of the dining room.

"Well, who should we talk to today?" Brian's question to Tom brought forward a list with eight names.

"You'll notice I underlined the ones I thought may be more beneficial." Tom pointed to three names. "The master sergeant is the motor pool sergeant for this base. You'll find him at the motor pool or the NCO club." He looked around slowly before continuing. "The other two are with the Army National Guards aviation company out of Holman Field in St. Paul."

"Why those individuals? I would think that our victim would be more closely aligned with men of his own rank." Brian looked down and studied the other people that made up the short list.

"That's easy; the three people I picked out are all full-time technicians, as was Frank. There is a bond among the techs that does not exist with strictly part-timers. Those three were particularly close to Frank and to Bascom. If anyone can help, those three would be able to."

"Fair enough." Brian looked around to make sure no one was within hearing. "Who's Wolf?"

"He's a maverick." Tom smiled at Brian in a form of acknowledgment for the homework the detective did in just two and a half hours.

"Great. What's a maverick?" Besides being mystified, Brian's mind was no longer in great shape, due to the denial of a necessary ingredient, sleep.

"A maverick is an enlisted man turned officer. Usually they are more prone to favor the men over the officer ranks, although sometimes they move up to general. Usually they are relegated to the middle management ranks and retire out as captain or major, at least on active duty." Tom stopped suddenly and motioned to Brian.

The three unit's officers paid their fees and took their place in the mess hall line. The major and both lieutenants were laughing and talking about something that no one except those standing near them could hear. Suddenly the commander pointed toward the first sergeant and smiled. Tom waved and returned the smile, at the same time mumbling, "I hope the SOB doesn't sit with us."

"I think we'll carry out our serious conversation later," was Brian's total reply.

Detective Sergeant David Brokowsky opened the door to the Hidden Place Lounge on Third and Hennepin, took a deep breath, and stepped into the dark interior. It took a full thirty seconds for his eyes to become accustomed to the dim lighting. Approaching the bar, he passed a small dance floor and a number of tables surrounded by soft, overstuffed chairs. Along the walls were posters of famous (and not-so-famous) movies, all indicating subtly the type of clientele that frequented this exclusive, expensive night spot.

The bartender and his four patrons stopped all conversation when Brokowsky entered the bar and, watching from their respective seats, waited for the detective to arrive at their position. Brokowsky wished Brian was with him on this most important call.

The bartender's smile was one of those imitation grins that make most individuals cringe with a feeling that borders on disgust. It gave the newly-arrived detective a feeling that if he happened to shake the bartender's hand, he should count his fingers twice for safekeeping.

"Hi. How can I help you?" The expression sounded about as sincere as a con man in a revival tent.

"I'm Detective Sergeant Brokowsky." Dave flipped his ID open so that all could see that this was an official visit. "I would like to ask you a few questions in private."

Two of the four customers finished their drinks and immediately left the establishment. The other two sat with their eyes fixed on the bartender, awaiting his response.

"Shoot, Officer…this is as private as we're going to get." The bartender turned and refilled his customer's drinks. "On the house," he announced, as he began to wipe his hands.

"Have you ever seen this man?" The picture that Brokowsky tendered to the bartender was one of those black-and-white photos of the deceased's head and shoulders that the police crime unit so carefully staged for its collection.

"Boy, this picture does no one justice." The bartender slid the picture to his two customers for their look-see. "I've seen him in here a couple of days a week."

"So you got a name to go with your identification?" Brokowsky's first impression about the man behind the smile was beginning to grow.

"I think his name was Harry something or other. We don't pay much attention to names in here because most of our customers don't use the ones their parents gave them, for obvious reasons, of course." The bartender began wiping the wetness from a perfectly dry bar.

"Why do you want to know?" The younger of the two remaining patrons, a boy who appeared to be no more than seventeen or eighteen, spoke up.

"He was murdered last week, and we're trying to find the killer." The answer was blunt and meant to shake the three, yet it did no more than bring a denial of knowledge from the young one and a shrug from the older patron.

"Did you know where he lived or what he did for a living?" The question was one that Brokowsky did not expect to receive a helpful answer to, so the response surprised him.

"Yeah. He claimed to work out at the airport and he said his pad was over in St. Paul somewhere." The bartender paused to think. "At least that's where I think he said he lived, but then maybe I'm wrong."

Dave studied the bartender. He could not bury the feeling that he was lying…but why? "Is that all you know?"

The bartender shook his head yes and went about wiping the dry bar top.

"How about a lover? Did he have one?" Brokowsky studied the man's motions in response to the question.

"I can't remember him having a steady." Once again, the bartender began to wipe down the bar. "I think he was the type who liked variety."

"Okay. Was he in here last Thursday evening?"

"Thursday evenings are pretty busy…in fact, almost as busy as Friday and Saturday."

The bartender began wiping again. "I think he was in for a short time, maybe an hour." He wiped some more. "Yeah…he came in about 6:00 p.m., had two, maybe three drinks, and left around 7:30."

"Okay. Did he leave with anyone?" Brokowsky began to watch the bartender's facial expressions.

"To tell you the truth, I couldn't say." He looked at the middle-aged businessman. "John, you were here. Can you remember seeing this guy?" The bartender was obviously trying to shift the questioning to someone else.

"No," came an almost shouted response. "Never saw him, nor do I ever remember seeing him at any time. If you remember, I didn't get here till almost 8:00 p.m."

"That's right. You must have got here just after he left." The bartender looked directly at the detective. "I think that's about all I can tell you."

"Well, thank you for your attention. I may be back later. By the way, what's your name?"

"I'm Gerald Bradshaw. They call me 'Jerry.' I'll be here every day, except Sunday and Monday—those are my days off."

Brokowsky walked slowly out of the lounge, thinking that he should get back and question the bartender more. *Oh well.* He shrugged his shoulders. *This confirmed the military. Bascom was a queer and probably got killed by a lover. Case closed.* He smiled to himself. Yet thoughts about the bartender persisted all the way back to the station.

Brian finished the questioning at the unit at eleven in the morning. From there, he drove over to the motor pool. The master sergeant, NCOIC of the motor pool, shook his hand and bid him a seat.

Smiling from across the desk, the sergeant opened the questioning. "I've been expecting you. What would you like to know about Harry Bascom?"

"Things sure get around on this base." Brian only received the printed list just fifteen minutes ago, and this sergeant already knew he was coming. "Did Sergeant Mullins let you know I was coming?"

"No. You have to remember that you're on a military base. We have a very closed society. When anything happens or when there is a stranger on the base, the word gets around almost as soon as it occurs or that stranger arrives." He sipped his coffee. "In your case, the grapevine reported your presence yesterday, and I put two and two together and came up with me." He smiled. "Would you like a cup of coffee?"

"Sure. Make mine black." The sergeant turned toward his coffee pot and poured the black liquid into one of the cups that was apparently part of a small collection.

Brian admired the cup. "That's a beautiful cup. I have a collection myself."

"Yes sir. That's my pride and joy; it's got the West Point crest on one side and an impression of the ring for the class of '62 on the other side."

"Well, let's get right to the point. Tell me about Harry Bascom." Brian had brought a yellow legal pad with him. He flipped it open to an empty page.

"Fred is, or was, a member of the Knights of Columbus. He was an ardent church member and served as an altar boy for the various chaplains. He liked his women and had a steady girlfriend. They we're planning to get married sometime in August." The sergeant paused to refresh himself. "He was attending the University of Minnesota at night, and I think he was close to his degree. He looked after his mother when his father died and was a devoted son."

"In relation to his military career, I think you should talk to Tom about that. In fact, he can verify what I just told you." He stopped to light a cigarette.

"How come you know so much abut him when his duty station is about a hundred miles away?"

"Harry worked with me until about four years ago, when I moved up here from the cities and he moved over to the 1327th. I used to take classes with him, and I brought him into the Knights. The girl he was going to marry is my daughter. Any further questions?"

"Did you know of any reason that someone would want to kill Harry?"

"I'll answer that, but it's almost lunch time. Why don't you eat with me? We can walk over to the club from here."

"That's a good idea. I should eat something before I leave, and I should get some exercise. Let's go." Brian stood and held the door open for the sergeant.

A gentle rain started to fall as the two men began their short journey toward the NCO club. The cool breeze brought the temperatures plummeting down at least twenty degrees since the day before. It was typical of Minnesota, with its ever-changing weather patterns. The cold front hovered just south of Little Falls and threatened to dive toward the Twin Cities at a moment's notice.

"Detective, let me explain the facts of life in the military. First, you must never wash your dirty laundry in public. Second, you must never question the authority of your commanding officer. And third, always keep quiet on things you see that do not affect you. They are none of your business."

The sergeant began to smile. "Harry happened to join in about the only unit in the nation that has a section that is made up of enlisted people who were all college educated. In fact, the only person that has not graduated is the tower officer. Harry fit into the section and the unit because of his college training and because Tom Mullins has always allowed his people to think on their own."

"What's wrong with that?" Brian looked questioning at the sergeant.

"Nothing, if they can obey orders. The problem comes in when the orders are poor and the men know more than the officers. To the military, that can be a disaster. Few officers allow the men to input their ideas on a project, nor do they actively seek the men's opinions."

He grimaced before continuing. "The military cannot allow a democracy to occur; it functions better as a dictatorship."

Brian's face fell as he listened to the master sergeant explain the functioning of a military unit. They were halfway to the NCO club when the motor pool sergeant broke that train of thought and began to explain about Harry Bascom.

"Harry came up the week end before his death and we went over to the Legion for a beer. He was getting ready to write a letter to the inspector general on the problems he found in his unit. I warned him that such things eventually get out, and, once they did, his career would be over. Besides, a letter to the IG would warrant no investigation, as the occurrences he was relaying happened in the Guard, not on active duty."

The detective looked sideways at the sergeant before asking, "Was there anything said that could have gotten him killed?"

"That's what's got me worried and upset. He told me, and don't quote me on this, that there was a problem with twelve file cabinets that kept popping up every six or seven months in the MARS program. These file cabinets kept turning up as salvage and kept being…how did he say it…'recycled through the system.'" The sergeant paused now and looked as though he was questioning himself before making his next statement.

"Go ahead, sergeant. I know a little about the problem already." Brian waited as the two turned up the walk to the NCO club.

"There is a war in Southeast Asia. I've been there, and it's not pretty. One of the things that happen in a war is that an awful lot of people, some in the military, make a huge amount of money. In this war, it's the legal and the illegal. Theillegal, as always, is in black market sales of all kinds. This includes weapons." The sergeant paused before opening the door to the club. Glancing around, he finished his thoughts. "Learn about the drug trade, and you will probably be on to something."

Brian reached out and put his hand on the sergeant's arm, stopping him from opening the door. "What do you mean 'the drug trade'?"

"Detective, it's the biggest military secret around, and it's making a lot of money for an awful lot of people. I won't say any more, because I don't know that much. Needless to say, that's where I think you'll find the reason for Harry's murder. Talk to 'Wolf' if you want more information." With that, he opened the door and dropped the subject.

"Drugs?" Brian's question was more of a surprise reaction.

"See Tom Mullins." With that, the master sergeant entered the barroom and ordered two beers.

CHAPTER NINE

The drive to Brainerd took an extra fifteen minutes as Brian thought over his fourth meeting with Mullins. The first sergeant's explanation of why he did not tell him everything he knew about "Wolf" Anderson was understandable. The detective had a feeling that he was being sucked into a military affair against his will. He needed to contact Minneapolis and find out what they had on the missing supply sergeant, Frank Valencio. It was also time to talk to his partner about what he had discovered during the last two days.

Anderson must be an interesting character. From what the first sergeant said, the man was a real-life hero of the old school. He was someone who acted in the interest of society and not for themselves.

A short announcement of the name of a murder victim found Sunday at Balsam Lake startled Brian out of his daydream and brought him up short. The radio station's news at five moved on quickly to the latest from Vietnam, as Brian began to wonder if he had heard right. Another Guard sergeant had been murdered, and this one, according to Angel and Mullins, was last seen with Valencio.

Brian glanced out of his rearview window. A black Ford that had left the fort the same time he had was still following. *Probably going into Brainerd,* he thought. Brian was approaching the center of Brainerd, where he would turn right and head east to State Highway 25. He glanced again into the rearview mirror and signaled left as he pulled up to the traffic light.

The black Ford's left turn indicator flashed its warning a moment later.

The Ford followed him around the corner as he headed toward Paul Bunyon's amusement park on the west side of Brainerd. He turned north following 371 and began picking up speed as he watched his shadow follow at a respectful distance. His mind began to race as he realized that only his partner knew exactly where he was staying.

He allowed his speed to slowly increase to the sixty-five miles per hour as he began to pass North Long Lake. Just past the lake, he applied his brakes and made a sharp right turn. The black Ford followed him into the narrow, winding blacktop road. The bends for the next three miles allowed Brian to increase his speed enough to widen the gap just enough so that his car was out of sight of the Ford for short periods of time.

Three miles into the road it turned sharply to the left, and in the middle of that turn, a road shot off to the right. It was there that Brian turned, gunned his engine, and sprinted until the road turned and hid him from the intersection. The black Ford, not seeing Brian's turn, rushed past the intersection and continued to follow the winding road to the left around Round Lake. Brian smiled to himself as he visualized the driver and his passenger wondering which way to turn when he ended back on 371.

Brian reached the second curve and shot around it, taking up his eastbound travel. When the black government vehicle reached 371, the driver realized that Brian had left the road they were on before they had reached 371. The passenger remembered the intersection where Brian had turned and urged the driver to go back to that turn. On reaching it, the Ford raced at ninety miles per hour down the two-and-half-mile stretch. The driver braked just as it entered the ninety-degree turn at a speed too high to sustain the turn. Like a missile, the Ford met the oncoming trees with brakes screeching. Too late, the occupants felt their bodies crumble as their vehicle dissolved in the hardwood forest. Brian drove a few more miles before pulling into the parking lot of the small bar, bait, and gas station at the top of the "Y." From there, he could enjoy a cool beer while he watched the approaches and made his telephone calls. While he felt relatively sure that he had shaken his shadow, he began to have second thoughts about the safety of his family.

His first call went to his partner in Minneapolis. Brokowsky answered in his usual gruff way only to brighten up when he heard his longtime partner's voice intone, "God, I wish you'd brighten up that greeting," Brian said. The standing joke around headquarters was a threat to shift Brokowsy to answering phones and thereby cut business by 100 percent.

It was 8:00 p.m. when Tom Mullins put on a clean set of fatigues, walked over to the military pickup, started up the vehicle, and drove the short distance to downtown Little Falls. The town had two major enterprises during the summer months: tourists seeking the home of Charles Lindberg, the "Loan Eagle," and catering to the whims of the citizen soldiers who trained at the Guard base some five miles north.

Angelica Valencio stepped outside the hotel at precisely 9:00 p.m. She had stayed in her room all day, per Tom's instructions, venturing out only when the darkness of night had finally settled in. The prearranged meeting would accomplish two things: it would allow them both to go over any information that they might have missed and would give Tom a chance to escort Angel back to St. Paul.

During the summer months, it was common for military vehicles to be seen traveling back and forth between Little Falls and Minneapolis, St. Paul. Highway 10 was relatively free of traffic on Tuesday night, as the majority of the boat-towing citizens had launched their boats the previous weekend and were safe in their rented or owned cabins, sipping drinks with friends. Tom calculated that he would be able to drive to St. Paul and back in about five hours. This would put him back at Ripley at about 3:00 a.m.

Tom swung his vehicle into the side street next to the church and waited. Five minutes went by before he heard a light tap on his rear window. He opened the passenger side and Angel slipped quietly into the seat. Slowly he pulled the pickup away from the curb and smoothly increased his speed to a safe twenty miles per hour. He swung around the block and joined the traffic on US Highway 10 going southeast.

The ride as far as Anoka was uneventful. He stopped in Big Lake to gas up and observed the traffic. No one seemed to be following. His next stop was in Anoka, where he pulled into a cafe parking lot. He and Angel entered the grill and, taking a table overlooking the street, they ordered coffee and rolls.

"Alright, Angel. How about bringing me up to date?" Tom had been surprised when Angel had shown up in Little Falls but did not pry into the reasons other than the disappearance of Frank. Now it was time for her to let him in on what had transpired since she had been notified of her estranged husband's disappearance.

"Tom, don't get excited, but after I was notified that Frank was missing, Teresa and I went over to the house"—she paused momentarily—"and discovered everything was trashed."

"What do you mean 'trashed'?" Tom's look sent a chill down her spine.

"Everything...all the furniture was destroyed, the bookshelves were overturned, the knick-knacks were crushed on the floor. I mean everything." She sobbed, thinking of the destruction.

"Did you call the police?" Tom's face showed his growing concern for his best friend's wife.

"Yes, for what little good that it did." It was more a frustrated statement than an attack on the police.

"Okay. Who did the police say did it?" Tom began to jump ahead to a conclusion he did not like to contemplate.

"The deputy. It was the Dakota County sheriff's department. Did I tell you that?" She looked up and answered her own question. "Sorry, Tom. Everything is happening so fast that I'm a little confused." She sipped her coffee before going on.

"The deputy thought it was teenagers out for a thrill."

"What do you think?" Tom suspected that the files were the prime motive, yet he wanted to hear it from someone else. Call it confidence building.

"The teens in the neighborhood all liked Frank. I think they were looking for the files and decided to make it look like a teenage act of violence." Angel once again began to quietly sob.

Tom agreed. "I think you're right and, furthermore, I think you're in danger along with anyone who has any knowledge of what is going on." He paused for only a moment. "Angel, where are you staying?'

"With Teresa." Angel continued, "Her telephone number is unlisted, her last name is not on the lease nor the telephone and"—Angel smiled to herself—"we have the live-in protection of a German shepherd."

"Angel, if it's who or what I think it is, they will find you." Her eyes took on a look of fear as Tom plunged on. "You know that the military is involved somehow."

Tom glanced out the window and watched as an Air Force staff car drove past the cafe. He made a mental note of the number and breathed a sigh of relief when the car continued straight ahead.

"Let's get going." Tom paid the bill as Angel disappeared into the lady's room.

The Air Force staff car cruised by, going in the opposite direction. Tom glanced hurriedly around and spotted the rear exit.

He caught Angel's arm as she exited the "Queen's" door and rushed her toward the exit. Slowly he opened the door and, seeing it was clear, they ran to the olive, drab vehicle parked in the shadows of the building.

Brian sat in the front room of the rented cabin and thought about his next move. It was almost 10:00 p.m., and his wife and children were sleeping peacefully. He thought back to the early evening and felt sure that he had lost his tail, if that was what it was. He had seen ambulances and the police going toward that winding back road, but there had been no reports of accidents on the news.

Wednesday he would take the chance and, leaving his family at the cabin, he would travel to Minneapolis and see what was going on. He had a feeling that his partner was doing as little as possible so as not to make waves. His dual positions did not speak well for this particular case. One could not blame the man; he had some fifteen years total military service. He had certainly earned his direct commission since joining the ranks of congressional gentlemen and he tried doubly hard to prove himself.

The softly playing music on the radio was interrupted by the ten o'clock news. Brian turned up the sound ever so slightly. The short announcement confirmed his belief that he had lost his followers. "The bodies of two men were found in the wreck of a black Ford on Crow Wing County 127. They were traveling at a high rate of speed and had missed a hairpin turn. No other information is available." Brian switched off the radio.

Brian finally took himself to bed for a few hours' rest. Morning comes all too early in these northern woods. His wife would be upset, but even she was beginning to understand the nature of the case he was working on. He would return Wednesday evening and spend the rest of the week enjoying his much-needed summer vacation.

Tom Mullins rolled up to the non-discreet apartment building in St. Paul; he had made it from Camp Ripley in three hours. He helped Angel down and carried her overnight case into the apartment. Once again he studied the street to make sure no other traffic had followed them.

"Tom, why don't you let me fix you a cup of coffee?" Tom felt that Angel had something else to tell him, and he did not want to break away quite yet.

Teresa answered the door with the German shepherd held closely at her side. After an introduction, the dog allowed this stranger to enter and sit in the corner chair where he could keep an eye on him.

"Tom, Teresa and I have another box full of documents. We don't know just what is in it, nor would we understand their meaning if we opened it." She stopped now and awaited his response.

"Where is it?" Tom hoped they did not have it in the apartment.

"It's still where we found the first box," Teresa intoned. "Neither my mother nor I could reach it."

Tom looked at Angel, hoping she would let him know where the hiding place was.

Angel smiled, poured a cup of coffee, and sat opposite Tom. "Tom, if you go to my house and go to its left side, you will find a crawl space under the house. The box is hidden in that crawl space."

Tom laughed. "No wonder the housebreakers couldn't find them." He turned serious now and, looking directly at Angel, said, "I think I'll pick them up tonight and make sure they're put someplace where we can get them without raising too much attention" He smiled again. "After all, prowling around a house late at night should not create a problem with the sleeping neighbors."

Angel looked at Teresa, who nodded in agreement. "Get it done, Tom."

"Consider it done." Tom, with a glance at the now-alert shepherd, said his good night and left by the rear exist.

The knocking on the cabin door began at midnight. Brian, in a sound sleep, lay there attempting to remember just where he was and what the noise was. His wife turned on her side. "Brian, someone's at the door."

He gradually aroused himself, standing in the dark. He began to feel his way toward the door. One more knock. "Okay, I'm coming!" he shouted out. He hoped that he didn't wake the children. Just then, he hit his shin on a kitchen chair. "Damn," he exclaimed as he stumbled on.

The resort owner stood on the porch, getting ready to knock one more time, when Brian threw open the door. "I'm sorry to wake you. You have an urgent phone call up at the lodge." The owner looked about as sleepy as Brian felt. "He would not leave a message and insisted I wake you."

"Wait till I put some clothes on." He turned on the front porch light and used that to retrieve his pants and shirt from where he had thrown them the night before. Slipping into his slippers, he whispered to his wife, turned, left the cabin, and made his way to the lodge.

"Detective, this is Tom Mullins." The voice of the first sergeant came over the line loud and clear.

"This better be good, top," he said, using a marine expression he'd picked up in the corps.

"I've just retrieved another file from Frank's house. I think it will tie together with the file we already have." He stopped now for a breath of air and waited for the detective to respond.

"Where are you?" Brian thought that Tom was at Camp Ripley, but if he had just retrieved a file from Valencio's home, it meant he had to be in St. Paul.

Mullins was quiet for a few seconds. When he finally spoke, Brian could just barely make him out. "Right now I'm at a gas station in St. Paul. I would like to turn these files over to you as soon as possible, because I've got to get back to the base."

"It's 11:00 p.m. right now. You won't get here till about two or three in the morning. Why don't you keep them with you until tomorrow, and I'll meet you at Ripley?" Brian hoped Tom Mullins would agree.

There was a long pause as Tom thought Brian's suggestion over. "Brian, I'll tell you what...I'm going to stop at the Greyhound bus depot in Little Falls and use a lock box for overnight, that way I won't have to bring the files on base. I'll see you tomorrow."

CHAPTER TEN

Brokowsky looked at his image in the mirror and didn't like what he saw. He was playing a game on the "Guard Murder," as it was beginning to be called by the press. Such a game did not rest easily on his Catholic conscience. His third grade teacher, Sister Matilda, would have questioned the ethics of his decisions and would not have approved He applied the Brut shaving cream his girl liked so much. He began the slow strokes with the razor that would smooth his face and refresh him all at the same time.

Finishing his shave, Dave reached for the phone with the intention of calling his partner. He thought better of it and slammed the phone back on the cradle. *Damn,* he thought. Every time he tried to play the game, he found Sister Matilda questioning his morals and his ethics. The woman had been dead ten years. Her funeral had been sort of a reunion with over five hundred of her former students in attendance. It's strange how this simple nun had touched so many lives and left such an indelible mark on her charges.

He finished dressing and left his apartment. The trip to downtown would only take about fifteen minutes. He decided to dig deeper into Bascom's background.

Dave arrived at 8:00 a.m., just as his partner called. "Brokowsky." His telephone answering technique remained the same.

"Dave, it's Brian. I'm in Foley gassing up and I should be in about ten. Let's go over everything we've got." Brian was in a hurry and was about to hang up when Dave suddenly responded.

"Brian, let me check that bartender out again, and do me a favor,"—he did not wait for a response—"stay out of the office for now and call me again about four."

Before Brian could utter another word, Dave's next comment brought a smile to his face. "Sister Matilda advised me to stop playing games and let the chips fall where they will."

His partner had finally decided to press for the right answers and stop trying to be two things at once. "Okay, partner. Whatever you say." With that short answer, Brian hung up.

He wondered about Dave's seemingly worried message. He continued to the cities to see if he could find "Wolf" Anderson.

Dave reviewed everything he had on the case. He paused every so often to think through a problem and make a correction to his notes. It was 11:00 a.m. when he stood, stretched, and left the station. The doors should be open at the Hidden Place Lounge.

The bar was dark when he entered, and it took time for the detective's eyes to become accustomed to the dim light. There were three people sitting at the bar with the bartender of Dave's previous acquaintance in attendance.

"Officer, what can I help you with?" The bartender greeted Dave almost friendlily. Two of the patrons began to stand when Dave put a hand on the younger one's shoulder.

"Stay put, and let's sees your ID." Dave was looking squarely at the younger of the two. "I don't think you're old enough to be in here."

"Officer," the bartender intervened, "I asked him for his driver's license just before you came in." The bartender looked toward the third patron, who had not moved from his seat.

"Okay then, get the ID out." Dave's eyes shifted to the third party. He looked to be about thirty-five and six feet tall. He was dark-skinned and slim, weighing maybe about 165 pounds. His crew cut gave him a military look, and his face indicated someone had been through more than his share of mayhem. The third man stared directly at Dave, whose spine suddenly felt a chill.

The look that the bartender had given him had a closeness in it that indicated he was more than just a customer. Detective Brokowsky didn't like this apparent friendship between this third party and the bartender.

Dave reached for the ID that the youngster handed him. Sixteen was right. Dave turned now toward the bartender, his voice growing hard. "Bartender, that's a drink at the spot where this young man is seated. Now, if you'd like, I can cite you for serving a minor." He waited for a response, his eyes glancing over the patrons.

"Officer,"—the third customer had found his voice—"I think you should back off for now."

Dave looked again at this unknown man. He was a hard case and, Dave could tell by sizing him up quickly, not an individual to contend with when one had no backup. "May I have you're name, sir?"

"Sure, Officer. My name is James Johnsen, and I'm a friend of the owner." He paused before continuing. "I saw the bartender ask for the young man's ID and refuse to serve him. The drink in front of him is mine; the bartender put it down there as you came in." He then quickly reached over taking the drink.

"Okay" Dave said, now may I have a chat with you?" He was looking directly at the bartender. "Privately, of course."

The bartender shook his head yes and, asking his friend to take his place, entered a rear room.

The office was done in a tasteful red and gold. A plush, gray rug lent itself to the black leather, overstuffed couch, and chair. The walnut desk detracted from the rest of the room. It was a large, executive style. Its top formed a counter across the sides and front so that anyone sitting in one of the matching side chairs could pull up to the desk as though they were at a table.

"Okay Detective, let's have it. My time is valuable." The bartender took a seat in the large executive chair behind the desk. He was obviously more than a bartender—possibly the owner or partner.

"I'm impressed at your color scheme." Dave took a wild guess. "This must have been a Chinese restaurant at one time."

"Right. Now stop wasting my time and get on with it, whatever it is." The bartender or owner appeared to be slightly nervous.

"The last time I was in, I asked about one Harry Bascom." Dave watched for the expression on the bartender's face. "That day you indicated that Harry would come in a couple of times a week and that on Thursday, the week before my visit, he was here from 6:00 p.m. to 7:30 p.m. Is that correct?"

"If I said it, that's right." The bartender looked a little shaken by the question, and it was obvious that he was attempting to shortcut the answer.

"Okay. Those couple of times a week, just what days were they?" Dave had suspicions about the story. Just maybe he could trip the bartender up.

The bartender thought for a while before speaking. "He was a regular on Thursday night, usually coming in about 7:30 and staying till the place closed." He paused again and then continued.

"He varied his second day, but never came on Saturday or Sunday. I think it was usually on Monday."

"Are you sure about those days? This is very important." Dave wanted to hear it one more time.

"Yeah. Always on Thursday nights and one other night that varied." Looking right at Dave, the bartender continued, "If that's it, I've got to get back to my customers. It's the noon rush." With that, he opened the door to the bar and held it open for Dave to precede him.

The bar was now almost half full. Most of the patrons were men, although there were two women sitting by themselves in a back booth. More patrons were entering the main entrance when Dave took his leave and left the bartender and his friend conversing quietly at the end of the bar.

Frank Valencio awoke to a buzzing noise coming from the bathroom. Glancing around, he guessed it was about noon. He struggled into a sitting position and reached for the crutches leaning against the wall. His broken leg had been set by a doctor friend of the retired Sergeant Major Emmett Massey.

Massey and Frank went back some thirty years. Both had been in the Army Guard when the Roosevelt call-up began. "So long, dear. Be back in a year," was the saying. The call-up for them went from June of 1941, to November, 1945. Massey had stayed on active duty.

When Frank had been called up again in 1950 for Korea, he again served with Massey—this time as a replacement. After Korea, Massey had again stayed on active duty while Frank had taken a discharge and re-enlisted in the Air National Guard. Massey then served in early Vietnam upon returning stateside.

He had taken his pension after twenty-five years on active duty and five years in the Guard.

The buzzing stopped, and Emmett came out of the bathroom holding an electric razor. His perpetual five o'clock shadow had been partially shaved away. He looked at Frank, standing precariously on his crutches, and smiled. "Can't keep a good man down." This was his only statement as he proceeded to set the table for the brunch he had prepared.

"Well, Frank, how about filling me in?" The sergeant major did not like to mince words. He had dropped everything to pick Frank up at Clear Lake. The old man had helped him put a temporary splint on Frank's broken leg. The old man's wife and the neighbor had helped Emmett put him in the back of his pickup and cover him with a tarp.

The ride to the doctor's office was excruciating but necessary. Doctor Smith was an old friend of Emmett's and had not asked any questions. He fixed the simple break and put on a proper cast. From there, Massey had helped Frank to his cabin and would put him up for who knew how long. It was now time for Frank to bring Emmett up to speed.

The serious expression on Emmett's face warned Frank not to try to evade the question. "Well, I'm not going to dance the side step on you, Emmett." Frank stopped before going on. He thought for a moment and then continued. "I drove to Ripley by VOCO of the commander."

"Okay, what did you do then?" Emmett wanted Frank to speed up his tale.

"I got to Ripley, and Tom talked to the commander, and he told Tom to get me down to Snelling immediately, if not sooner." Frank's face reflected a questioning look before he continued. "Major Spaulding said he had never given me a verbal order. When I arrived on base, I checked into my office and then went over to the club. Master

Sergeant Mike Swanson met me at the club. "He looked squarely at Emmett. "I think it has something to do with the death of Harry Bascom."

"I've been reading what little is in the paper about it." Emmett stopped and puffed on his pipe as he waited for more.

"Mike opened up the motor pool for me and I put the semi away. Then we returned to the club for a nightcap." Frank stopped to consider the night. "Mike's not a drinker, and I've been partly on the wagon, so we had two glasses of beer a piece and left the club about 1:00 p.m."

Emmett interrupted, "You didn't have any more than that, did you?"

"Heck no." Frank showed he was a little peeved at the question. "Well, we got in Mike's pickup and drove across the bridge to St. Paul. We noticed a car had followed us out of the parking lot on the base, but we didn't think much of it. We had just pulled up to my place when this car pulled in front of us and two men got out." Frank paused now as he tried to arrange his thoughts.

Emmett got up and reached for the scrambled eggs on the stove. "It's time to eat." He began dishing the brunch out. "Go ahead with your adventure while we're eating." To Emmett, everything was an adventure.

"They had guns and ordered us to get in the backseat of a car. It was a black Chrysler. Since you don't argue with a man with a gun, we immediately got into the car." Frank tried to scratch his leg, to no avail.

"Go on, Frank," Emmett urged.

"One got in the front seat, while the other man got into our truck and drove it off. A third man was at the wheel, and we drove off toward the base." As he recounted the story, Frank began to get a clearer picture of just what had occurred and possibly why.

"They entered the base at the gate closest to the old polo fields. That gate is normally padlocked, but it was open and no guard was on it." This was beginning to sound ridiculous.

Frank continued. "There was a helicopter parked in a field near the east side of the base. We were ordered in, and about that time, a second car drove up with a third man. He got out and joined us in the helicopter."

Emmett was beginning to worry about his friend's mental health. "Frank, are you sure you were on base, or did you get your directions mixed up?"

"No. I didn't get my directions mixed up, and we definitely were on the base." Frank looked directly at his friend. "Do you want to hear the rest of this crazy tale, or do you want to continue to interrupt?"

"Sorry, Frank. Keep going." The sergeant major looked down and studied his hands.

"We took off in the copter and headed northeast. About a half hour after take-off, we were about 3,000 feet over a lake, I think. In any case, you could see an outline of lights around a large open area. They started asking questions about files. They wanted to know what I knew about Harry Bascom." Frank felt a chill run up his spine as he began to think of four days ago.

"They kept asking while the copter kept circling that dark patch. Almost five minutes into this holding pattern, they got nasty and pulled Mike up to the open entrance." Frank paused and drank some coffee. So far, he had not touched his meal.

"The leader of the group asked me one more time what I knew about Bascom. When I said nothing, he pushed Mike out of the copter door. I still hear his screams as he fell to his death." Frank sobbed now and looked helplessly at the sergeant major.

"They had no reason…just plain cold murder. They just killed him and laughed about it." Frank's frustration and anger was contagious.

"Frank,"—retired Sergeant Major Emmett Massey had seen it all before—"take a minute and compose yourself." He looked out the window at the lake, its smooth water shining like glass in the warm spring morning. The peace of the scene belied the buried thoughts that were beginning to come to the surface. The story reminded him of the things that he'd seen in Nam, the reasons he had taken his retirement before his thirty years were up.

"Friend, the United States is not like you and I remember from the thirties and forties. The nation has changed and, unfortunately, the leaders have too. Well, I've said enough for now. Continue." Emmett forced a weak smile.

"Well, we proceeded northeast and started to put down on what appeared to be a complex of buildings. I could tell by the lights shining in the window. There were car lights shining on a small helicopter pad. We swooped down toward the pad and passed what looked like a swamp. When we got about twenty feet off the ground, I took a chance and jumped. I guessed I surprised everyone. The head man fired a couple of shots, and the helicopter climbed slightly." Frank once again paused for coffee.

"What happened next?" Emmett was beginning to become more and more interested.

"I landed pretty hard, but luckily on soft ground. I think I broke my leg on landing. The copter landed on the pad about 300 yards away. My adrenaline was really flowing. I got up and ran toward some woods. I could hear them yelling and the vehicle started to come toward me." Taking a deep breath, Frank continued his story. "I reached the woods and kept right on going like a bat out of hell."

"It was about three in the morning, and I stumbled through the woods till I literally stumbled into another swamp. By this time, I could hear voices coming from behind me. They were having trouble in the dark." Frank, for the first time, took a bite of food.

"I moved cautiously deeper into the swamp. It was pitch dark and the mosquitoes attacked unmercifully. I know that I had to put a lot of distance between me and my pursuers. I stopped at about four in the morning and rested on a small island in what I thought was the middle of the swamp."

He looked at his friend with eyes that reflected a confusion born of hatred and fear.

"Emmett, I don't know why this has happened unless it has to do with the fraud that Bascom and I found in the unit. But it's not worth killing someone for the little bit of money that's involved." Frank drank a little more coffee before finishing. "About five in the morning, I crawled toward a beach I could see about fifty yards from me. My leg began to bother me, and I must have passed out. You know the rest of the story."

"Finish your brunch." Retired Sergeant Major Emmett Massey sat back and puffed on his pipe. He had a strange sensation that this was somehow connected with the military and, heaven forbid, an intelligence agency. He thought about the fraud that Frank had mentioned. He knew he had to ask about it.

"I'd like to call my wife and daughter and let them know I'm okay," Frank suddenly blurted out. Emmett answered immediately, "No way. It's too dangerous for them and you."

At 4:00 p.m. Brian walked into the squad room looking for his partner. Dave, engrossed in his notes, did not see Brian until he sat at the desk opposite him. "We've got some inconsistencies in the bartender's statements." Dave handed his notes to Brian. "At our first interview, the bartender indicated that Bascom was at the bar from about 6:00 p.m. till just before 8:00."

Brian smiled and, looking at Dave, said, "That's impossible. I called his council before I came in and found out that he was an officer in the Knights of Columbus. Their meetings are on the first and third Thursday of the month. They last from 7:30 till 9:00 p.m., and he was engaged to be married."

"When I called the council, I was notified that he attended all of the meetings. But to prove it, you and I are going to drive out to his council and check the roster and the minutes."

"Brian, how do you know about the Knights of Columbus?" Dave was Catholic, but had fallen away.

"I am one . . . that is, I pay my dues, but I don't attend any of the meetings. Years ago I was active, and my dad was a Grand Knight. After he died, I just stopped going. Maybe, Brian thought to himself, he would get active again.

Dave smiled and grabbed Brian by the arm. "Partner, let's take a ride over to St. Paul and find out what the truth is."

CHAPTER ELEVEN

Tom Mullins checked his watch. It was almost time to make the rounds of the facilities. When that was completed, he would join the men at the chow hall and eat dinner. The trip back from St. Paul had gone fast. He was back on the base by 3:00 a.m. and fell to sleep immediately after he hit the sack. Apparently no one has missed him. Both file boxes were safe and sound at a friend's place in Little Falls. He would retrieve them later and find a safer place for them. He should turn them over to the detective, but he was afraid they would get lost in the bureaucracy.

He pulled up to the mobile tower located almost in the middle of the field. Climbing the five steps to the tower van, he looked up to see two controllers squeezed into the operator's position. The watch supervisor sat on the lower deck while his top assistant instructed a young airman in the intricacies of air traffic control. The young man was having difficulty, although there were only three aircraft in the pattern. Tom laughed and nodded to the supervisor. "How's it going, Jim?"

"Not too bad. We decided to give him some hands-on practice. How was your trip to St. Paul?" Jim spoke as though the trip was common knowledge.

The first sergeant looked shocked. "Where did you hear that?"

"In the orderly room. I was just passing by on the way out here when I heard the old man talking it over with his clerk." Jim's look showed a marked concern for the "top."

Tom grunted and shifted the conversation deftly away from the subject. "Did the mess hall get your chow out here?"

"Sure did. Thanks, Sarge." Jim liked the first sergeant because of his concern for the men.

"Good. I better get on my way; I've got to stop at GCA yet." Tom knew the men liked to bullshit a little on his daily visits, but today he was going to cut it short.

"How about some coffee?" Jim offered the usual cup and was surprised at his first sergeant when he refused it. He was sure in a hurry all of a sudden.

Tom's stop at the GCA unit would be just as short. He didn't know how the information had gotten to the commander until he remembered the Air Force staff car at the restaurant in Anoka. Somehow they, whoever *they* were, had spotted him and probably followed him to St. Paul. If that happened, he must somehow warn Angel and her daughter. But how could the major have known? He would go to the orderly room and mention the trip in an off handed way and see if it drew some comments.

No, he thought. That would tip his hand. It must come from the commander. Maybe they really didn't know where he was going but only surmised it was St. Paul. That was a more likely scenario. The first sergeant looked around and found himself in front of the GCA unit.

He sat in his motionless truck with the motor running. Suddenly a young airman appeared from the maintenance van, walked over to the truck, and handed the first sergeant a cup of coffee. "Have a nice day, First Sergeant." The young airman turned and returned to the van.

Detectives Dave Brokowsky and Brian Donnley entered the Knights of Columbus hall at 5:00 p.m. What normally would have been a half-hour drive ended up being one hour due to the rush hour. Since they were using Brian's car, they theoretically were not on duty.

Dave looked at Brian as they entered the bar. "Two tap beers, please." Brian's facial features reflected approval of his partner's choice.

"Do you have a card, sir?" The question was polite but firm.

Brian reached for his billfold. *I hope the card is there,* he thought, as he riffled through the folded leather envelope. After what seemed to be a full two minutes, Brian triumphantly pulled his Knights of Columbus traveling card out of the now-open and disarrayed wallet.

"Okay. Now if you will, just sign the book over near the door. I'll pour your beer." The bartender motioned toward a stand next to the door.

"Bartender, I'm Detective Brian Donnley and this is my partner, Dave Brokowsky. We're both from Minneapolis, and we would appreciate it if you could tell us where the manager is."

"You're speaking to him. My name is Martin." The manager reached over to shake their hands. "Welcome to Council 2532."

Brian smiled and was surprised at the firm handshake of the manager, who appeared to be about sixty-five years old. "Thanks. We're both from the homicide department, and we'd like to ask you a few questions about Harry Bascom."

"Harry was one of our most active members. I just posted his funeral notice on the bulletin board. It's tomorrow at 9:00 a.m. at St. Cecilia's," the manager volunteered.

"Thanks. We'll try to be there." Brian looked directly into the managers eyes. "How well did you know Mr. Bascom?"

"Ten years. He helped me every Monday and Thursday night. Monday he worked the bar himself, and on Thursday's he would spell me because of the bingo crowd. We get busy here on Thursday, Friday, and Saturday nights. We're closed on Sundays, except for a communion brunch for the members once a month and a Mother's Day brunch once a year."

Dave jumped into the conversation. "Not that we don't believe you, but we would like some actual proof. Did he make out a time card or anything else that would confirm what you just told us?"

"Sure, Officer. We'll show you the payroll sheet. Everybody that does anything around here is requested to sign." Martin turned and, opening a drawer, pulled out a yellow legal pad of paper. He handed it to Brian.

Brian laid the pad on the bar so that he and Dave could study it. It was a yellow legal pad with three hand drawn lines running vertically down the pad. Each line was separated by approximately two and a half inches. On the top of the column there were spaces for the activity and the date. For this pad, the activity was "Bar Help" and the date was left blank. Instead of using the top date space, someone had taken a ruler and, on the far left side, ruled a fourth vertical line in order to make a date column.

Martin saw the puzzled expression and volunteered, "I put down the date column because at any one time, we do not have more than two volunteers working here in the bar. You can see that the name is listed in the next column and columns for time-in and time-out."

Dave looked at Martin and blurted out, "You don't pay these people from this sheet, do you?"

Brian laughed as Martin looked at Dave with a smile that would do any Irishman proud. His grin was broad, his face lit up, and his eyes showed a twinkle that indicated an individual about to enjoy his next statement. "Sure. If the payroll sheet is good enough for God, it's good enough for man."

Dave looked up from the pad sharply and stared at Martin. "Don't give me that God stuff. I want to know if you pay off this payroll sheet."

"No,"—Martin paused only for a moment—"only God does."

Dave looked like a man ready to blow his stack when Brian, still laughing, interrupted. "Martin is pulling your leg, man; they don't pay money off these payroll sheets." Brian now looked at Dave and saw he was cooling off rapidly. "God pays in the afterlife. These are strictly volunteers—no cash pay involved."

"The payrolls, or what others call a sign-in sheet, are used by the council to make their reports to the national once a year." Martin was now explaining the reasoning behind the sign-in sheets. "Each work-project or volunteer effort that a knight takes part in has its equivalent of the sign-in sheet"

"Now," Martin went on, "for each project, we establish a sign-in sheet that allows us to compile the hours our people accumulate during the year, and these are sent to the national on our annual report."

"Consequently,"—Brian got in to the instruction—"in the Knights of Columbus, there is a sign-in sheet or payroll, as the fourth degree call it, for all meetings or volunteer efforts.

Martin took over. "Of course, if you're an officer, as Harry Bascom was, you will be noted as present in the minutes, and times are available for when you got here and when you left."

"Have you got the sign-in sheets for the last"—Dave thought for a moment—"oh, say…six months?" *You might as well clear Bascom's name while you're at it,* he thought.

"You'll have to see the financial secretary for everything past last Saturday. I keep Sunday to Saturday and turn them in on Saturday night when he comes by about 10:00 p.m." Martin smiled and looked at his watch. "The financial secretary has a meeting of the home association tonight; he'll be here in about half an hour. Why don't you stay around? I'm sure he'll get them out of the safe for you."

Brian took a sideways glance at his partner. "What the hell, partner? We're off duty; let's have two more beers while we wait."

"Brian, you talked me into it, but this time, I'm buying." Dave placed two dollars on the bar top. Martin poured the beer and gave fifty cents in change.

Command Sergeant Major Emmett Massey parked his car in front of the 1327th orderly hut and entered the building with a confidence only reflected by those used to command. His slim six-foot frame was adorned with his summer class-A uniform. The ribbons on his breast reflected every action that the United States Army had fought in from 1941 to 1968.

His personal awards included a Silver Star, two Bronze Stars, two Purple Hearts, a Meritorious Service Medal, three commendation medals, and the soldier's medal. Just above the ribbons was the combat infantry badge. A paratrooper's wings glistened at the top of his awards. The foreign awards told everyone in the know that this was a man who had fought not only in World War II, but in Korea and Vietnam.

Emmett had felt a little self-conscious about putting on his uniform. Frank and he had discussed it at length and felt that no lower enlisted member of the National Guard would even think about questioning a sergeant major with all of that fruit salad. More importantly, it would help him bluff his way through any tough spots, on the outside chance someone tried to question his presence.

Airman Second Class Thomas William Trent looked up from his duties and gasped. The soldier entering his office had more ribbons than any man he had ever seen. His strips indicated at least a master sergeant, if not higher. His appearance was immaculate, with each press in his uniform conforming exactly to the regulations. Since the sergeant was Army, Airman Trent assumed he had the wrong location.

"May I help you, Sergeant?" Trent's attitude reflected a superiority that bordered on arrogance. College educated draft evaders. Frank had told him about this very person.

"Is this the 1327th Air Traffic Control Flight, Airman?" Sergeant Massey spit out the word "airman" as though it left a bad taste in his mouth.

Trent immediately saw and felt the contempt in the use of the word. It was time to retreat. After all, he wanted nothing to hinder his up-and-coming direct commission. Once he received his second lieutenant bars, he could take care of these ignorant, undereducated NCOs.

"Yes, sir!" Trent's use of the word "sir" was intended as an outward show of respect.

"Don't call me 'sir,' airman. I'm Command Sergeant Major Massey. To you I'm simply 'Sergeant Major.' Now can you direct me to your first sergeant?" Massey's voice was kept low, yet loud enough to instill fear in any mortal standing close enough to hear.

The airman spoke nervously, "Yes s . . . sir . . . I mean, Sergeant Major. Sergeant Mullins is on his rounds. He called from the GCA unit just about five minutes ago. He was on his way to the maintenance hut."

"And where, pray tell, is your maintenance hut?" The sergeant major continued to keep his verbal pressure on.

"Out the door, Sergeant Major. Turn left and go two huts down. I would expect Sergeant Mullins will be there in about five minutes." Trent hoped this would get rid of his nemesis.

"Thank you, airman." Massey had made the last "airman" sound almost praising.

The sergeant major made an about-face and marched out of the orderly room door just as Tom Mullins pulled his pickup vehicle into the area parking lot. Spotting an individual in a class-A uniform bedecked with ribbons just leaving the orderly room with clipboard in hand gave Tom an early warning.

Tom went straight toward the maintenance hut where he had seen the Army sergeant major disappear. Entering the hut, he found Sergeant Major Massey introducing himself to the maintenance chief, Master Sergeant Henry Schmidt.

"Excuse me, Sergeant Major, I'm senior Master Sergeant Thomas Mullins, the first sergeant. Can I help you?" The sergeant major turned, and at that instant, Tom Mullins immediately recognized the bosom buddy of Frank Valencio.

"Yes, you can. I'd like to talk to you about a number of problems that the general has asked me to check on." Emmett's wink indicated a very different discussion would take place.

"Let's take a walk, Sergeant Major. I'm sure you and I can solve these problems between us." Tom had last seen Massey at Fort Bragg when he retired. That would have been two years ago. He had gone out there with Frank specifically for the retirement ceremonies and party afterward. It was there that he had learned that Emmett Massey had enlisted in the Army National Guard at the age of seventeen in 1936. When the call-up occurred in June of 1941, he had simply stayed on active duty,

"Yes, First Sergeant, I'm sure we can." He glanced at the maintenance chief and, looking at Tom, said, "I'm Emmett Massey. Glad to meet you."

Leaving the area, they headed across a field toward the mess hall. "Been a couple of years since we've seen each other, Tom."

"Sure has. By the way, I suppose you've heard about the disappearance of Frank Valencio."

"Yes. In fact, you could say that I've got the big picture firsthand." Emmett looked at Tom to see his expression.

"Sergeant Major, I'm not used to beating around the bush,"—Tom returned Emmett's look—"so let's cut to the chase."

"By golly, Frank said I would like you. For your information only, I just left Frank about one hour ago. He was sitting in an easy chair overlooking a lake and, except for a simple fracture of his right leg, he's okay." Emmett smiled broadly and waited for Tom's response.

"What happened? And can I tell Angelica? She and their daughter have been worried sick."

"I don't know if you should tell them immediately or not. I think he's in a very serious position. From what he tells me, there is an awful lot going on, and I, for one, don't like it at all. It smells too much like Nam." Both sergeants grew silent. They each began to ponder the quagmire they both found themselves in.

Brian Donnley and Dave Brokowsky found the financial secretary to be well-informed and sociable. More importantly, he offered proof that Harry Bascom could not have been anywhere but at the Knights of Columbus Hall that fateful Thursday night. At 10:30 p.m., Harry said he had to leave to meet someone.

There were at least fifteen witnesses, and unless you wanted to accuse a district judge of lying, Harry Bascom was present and accounted for from the hours of 6:30 p.m. to 10:30 p.m.

Dave and Brian decided to have one more glass of beer before leaving—Dave for his apartment and Brian for the "up north" of Minnesota fame.

"Someone wants us to file this case away and chalk if off as another homosexual killing." Dave kept his voice low so as not to be overheard by the five or six people that lined the bar.

Brian agreed. Of course, Brian smelled something rotten when he first looked at the deceased's wallet. It was Dave that needed to be persuaded.

"Let's assume that someone higher up wanted to cover up something." Brian smiled at Dave's frown before plunging on. "And let's assume further that there is some fraud...say money and equipment."

Dave did not like the direction his partner was leading, but Brian had spent at least two days at Camp Ripley. Just maybe… he probably did have more than Dave. "Okay, Brian, what have you got that I don't have?"

Emmett Massey finished telling Tom Mullins the condition of Frank and about the killing of the motor pool sergeant. The similarity of the incident to some of the eliminations in the Phoenix program disturbed the sergeant major. It appeared that problems just surfacing in Vietnam were similar to what was beginning to happen in the States. If that were the case, and that was a big *if*, there had to be more to it than some misappropriation of equipment or even a theft of a small amount of money. Emmett spelled out his thoughts to Mullins and warned the sergeant to be careful.

On Mullins's part, he quietly advised Massey of the existence of two files and promised to move them to a safer location as soon as practicable. "Sergeant Major, if anything happens to me, tell Frank his files are with Mousy. He'll understand."

"You know, Tom, I think we had better tell someone higher up about what our suspicions are."

"Sergeant Major, I think you had better handle that. I know a few people, but I think you probably have more connections than any of us." Tom stopped near the mess hall entrance, his expression giving away his worried state. "Yes, I think you should be extremely careful."

"You're right, of course. What about that detective? Maybe he should be brought up-to-date."

Mullins smiled at the thought of Brian Donnley. "You're right. Of course. I'll do that either tonight or tomorrow."

"Okay, Tom. You contact your detective and bring him up to speed. I'll go though my book and see if I can find someone we can trust. I'll talk to you before I do anything else. Meanwhile, don't tell Angel or her daughter about Frank." Massey was beginning to feel the old excitement flow through his scarred and battered body frame.

Tom smiled and, shaking Massey's hand, said good-bye. Watching the sergeant major walk...no, *march*, toward the parking lot gave him a sense of well-being. *Just maybe we'll get through this in one piece.*

Emmett Massey, smiling broadly, climbed into his pickup truck and leisurely drove off the base.

Dave Brokowsky opened the outside door of the Knights of Columbus hall to allow his partner to pass though on the way to the parking lot. The call from Brian to his wife in Merrifield did not go too well. She had expected him back, and now he was making some excuse to stay over and go to a funeral. Brian had attempted to be diplomatic, but he knew that he was in big trouble.

The information that Dave and Brian were now sharing proved that the bartender at the Hidden Place Lounge was lying. They now knew that there had been some theft, misappropriation of funds, and a second murder of a friend of the missing Frank Valencio.

They drove to within a block of Dave's apartment where Dave suddenly had second thoughts. "Brian, you go on up north, and I'll go to the funeral. Drop me off at the restaurant on the corner. I think I'll get something to eat."

"I think you're right. How about your car?" Brian thought he could drop his partner off at the parking garage across the street from City Hall.

"Don't worry about it. I'll get a bus to work and pick up the car tomorrow." Dave smiled at his partner. "Look's like we're finally making some headway."

Brian pulled his car up to the corner restaurant and smiled at Dave as he exited. "Have a good night, good buddy."

"Same to you, and be careful on your drive north." With that, Dave turned and entered the restaurant.

CHAPTER TWELVE

Jimmy Hendrickson swore, as he swung the wheel of his Ford pickup sharply to the right—too late. The vehicle hit the boulder head-on, punching a hole into the radiator.

"Jimmy, I told you not to go too fast on this dirt road." Bob Bosford, BB for short, spoke up for the first time since the vehicle had turned off the paved highway some three miles north of the two fisherman's current position.

The dirt road was supposed to lead them to a small, spring-fed lake. Fishing was presumed to be excellent. The problem came from the now-raging storm. Thunder and lightning lit up the evening, and any chance of reaching the campsite that bordered on the public access was now gone.

"I think it's time to take a walk." Bob was looking off in the direction they had just come from.

"You think that farmhouse will have a phone?" Jimmy peered at his radiator, realizing that it was time to call Triple A.

"It should, but it's about half a mile across that field." Bob flinched as the lightning lit up the early evening with another shock from the heavens.

"Well, let's get started." Jimmy and Bob began the long trudge toward the distant group of buildings.

Brian Donnley pulled his vehicle into the yard of his rented cabin and was greeted immediately by his son and wife. Her smile showed the pleasure that she felt in his deciding to return to the cabin.

Helen felt a tremendously warm feeling for this husband of hers. Sometimes he was like a little boy, wanting attention and doing some stupid things. At other times, he was strong and thoughtful. His steady hand was there always, guiding the children through their trials and tribulations, especially when he was needed.

Brian was glad to be in the protective cocoon of his family. His wife, although at times bitter because of his time at work, always accepted his devotion to his job. More importantly, she knew he had a deep, undying love for her and their children.

"How's the case going, dear?" Helen's question surprised him. It had been some ten years since she had ever asked him about any particular case.

Brian thought for a long minute before answering. "This case is different. From a simple homicide that everyone said was caused by a homosexual love triangle, it suddenly blossomed into a real mystery that might involve the military. Dave feels that he has enough to go to his military commander and suggest a serious investigation on the military end. I don't feel we have enough information."

Sensing his surprise at the questions, Helen quietly explained, "Honey, you have been so deeply involved with this case that I knew something was different. If you don't want to talk about it, I'll understand."

"No. It's not that I don't want to talk about it, it's that everything is in a state of flux." Brian took his wife's hand. "I think we'll drop it for now, at least till the solution becomes a little clearer."

Helen held her husband's hand and felt an outpouring of emotion toward this lovely individual. He had been on the force probably eleven years and had never drawn his gun. She smiled at him and kissed him lightly on the cheek. "Sweetheart, let's just have a drink here and watch the moon over the lake."

"Great idea. That's a lot better than any bar." Tom let himself relax and thanked God quietly for his blessings.

The farmhouse was dark when the two fishermen arrived on the front porch. At least, they thought, they were no longer plodding along in the rain. The porch gave them protection from the elements. Knocking on the door, the two men could not raise anyone. It was then that they noticed the barn door was swinging gently in the wind.

Running to the barn, they could just barely squeeze into the building. It was BB that brought out a flashlight. "My God," was the only exclamation from the two men as the light traveled over the boxes and crates packed inside the structure.

Bob was the first to speak after what seemed like an eternity. "Look at the military hardware. There's even a computer still in the crate."

"Yes!" Jimmy exclaimed. "Take a look at this—it's got a brand-new NCR computer in it."

The men became engrossed in a search through the wood crates and corrugated boxes. They immersed themselves in kind of a game to find something different and screamed out as they tried to outdo each other. Radio gear and electronic equipment could be found in every corner. Just as the two contemplated the climb to the rafters, they were brought to their senses by a crack of lightning so close that it shook the barn.

That action from the heavens brought them to a realization that they had stumbled into a warehouse full of what appeared to be stolen military gear. Their childlike enthusiasm evaporated and was just as suddenly replaced by a sense of fear and foreboding.

Jimmy was the first to speak. "I think we had better see about getting a hold of the sheriff."

"How?" BB was worried. "It's at least five miles to town, it's storming outside, and I don't see a telephone."

"Let's see if the house's back door is open or maybe one of the windows was left unlatched." Jimmy was already exiting the barn by the same way they entered.

Reaching the back porch, the men tried the door, only to find it locked. They split up and began to try all of the ground floor windows of the house. With the blinds drawn, they could not see what was inside.

On the fifth window they checked, the latch was open. The window did not want to open. With a little muscle from both men, the lower portion began to move ever so slowly.

Jimmy was the first to crawl inside. He found himself in the front room, surrounded by what appeared to be Victorian furniture of the first order. Sliding doors on the right and toward the back blocked his view of the rest of the home. He turned and helped BB through the small window. Crossing to the door, Jimmy flipped the light switch on. The light brought out the vivid colors in the murals that lined the walls. This room was special. It was like stepping back some seventy years to the turn of the century.

BB pushed open the sliding door only to find a hallway running about half the length of the house. In the hallway a few more boxes and one crate were visible. Directly opposite the living room entrance was another sliding door. Opening it, they found themselves in what appeared to be a former dining room turned into a partial office. A long table with eight chairs lined one side of the room. To the right, toward the window, sat a desk with an executive chair. A telephone sat invitingly in the middle of this oak expanse. Sitting at the desk, you could see the front yard and the driveway leading up to the house.

Jimmy reached out and picked up the phone. Dialing zero, he was immediately connected to the operator. "Operator, I'd like to talk to the sheriff."

Dave Brokowsky finished his dinner and slowly sipped a cup of coffee. The time was now 9:00 p.m., and the restaurant would soon close. He paid the bill, leaving a ten percent tip for the waitress. Sally, the owner, waved a cheerful good-bye as Dave stepped out the door.

As he crossed the street, he felt a sudden chill. He looked around and studied the street. No cars could be seen, nor were there any pedestrians. He walked toward his apartment house only to stop about one block away. There was something bothering him. He didn't know what, but something was wrong.

He turned now and began to walk toward Lake Street. He would walk till he got to that main thoroughfare and then approach his apartment from a different direction. He also decided to enter the building from the rear.

The sheriff and his deputy didn't know what to make of it. The two fishermen thought they should be charged with something. The call to the old Spalding place happened on the worst night of the year. Tornado warnings were out, severe thunder storm warnings, high wind, hail, and heavy rain were being forecast, and the night sure looked like it was going to live up to it's billing.

Jimmy, the more excitable of the two fishermen, explained the predicament they were in and had brought them up-to-date. The call to the judge produced a search warrant for the premises based on what was in the barn. The search had been going on for about

thirty minutes, with the deputy and BB beginning in the attic and the sheriff and Jimmy beginning on the first floor. The front room, kitchen, and part of the dining room, were being used as intended, the rest was a huge warehouse.

"I've seen enough." The sheriff's statement surprised the three others when they met on the second floor. "It looks like all military equipment, at least from the markings. That means it's a military problem, and I think I'm going to call the Minnesota Air National Guard in St. Paul and see what they think.

"You two," he said, looking first at Jimmy and then at BB, "get in the back seat of my car and the deputy and I will take you to town."

"Sheriff," the deputy spoke up, "do you want me to secure the premises?"

"Yeah, you better, and do it right." The sheriff again turned to the two fishermen. "We've got a pretty good motel on the edge of town, and we'll drop you off there. Okay?" He paused a minute and smiled. "I've always wanted to say this: Don't leave town without letting me know, okay?"

Both men nodded their agreement as all began to run toward the sheriff's car.

Retired Sergeant Major Emmett Massey opened the small black book that had been his bosom companion through some thirty-two years of soldiering. He leafed through the pages, stopping every so often to recall faces and places. His search of a name and address would be shorter than he realized. Many of the men he had served with were now gone, their places marked with a small gold star that he had carefully placed next to their names. The gold star had been the idea of his bride of some thirty-two years. She had died of cancer in the year he retired. He wiped away a tear and continued his search.

"Bingo!" The exclamation by the sergeant major shocked Frank out of a sound sleep.

Frank turned to look at the dial of the clock. "My God, Emmett, you've spent almost four hours on that book."

"Yeah, but did I find a good one…you betcha." Emmett tried to imitate a favorite expression of his Minnesota friend.

Frank laughed. "You still didn't get the "you betcha" right. You need some more practice."

"I think I found our man. He's a retired brigadier general serving at the Pentagon in a civilian status. He is an assistant secretary of the Army. I served with him in Korea and Vietnam. He's a good man who cannot stand fraud or waste. He considers such a thing as a pure and simple theft from the nation. In other words, a theft from the private citizens whose trust we need to protect the country." Massey paused for only a few seconds. "Well, Frank, what do you think?"

"You know him; I don't. All I can say is to be careful." Frank's eyes took on a sad look. "All I know is that sometimes the higher up you go, the less you can trust them."

"Well, just maybe we have to study the options more. If we decide to approach the general, maybe we should do a background check on him." Emmett looked expectedly at Frank.

"Background check? How are you going to accomplish that?" Frank's question made Emmett smile broadly.

"I have my connections, all of which aren't with the airborne." Emmett's eyes gleamed as he thought about another old friend of his in the FBI. Besides, this man owed him his life.

CHAPTER THIRTEEN

Dave Brokowski moved quickly across State Street and began to walk down a side street leading to his apartment some three blocks away. He checked a block ahead and behind and was sure that no one was following him, yet the weird feelings were still present. Seeing his corner bar, he stepped inside and ordered a Coke.

He sat there shooting the breeze with the bartender, a longtime friend, and collected his thoughts. He knew everyone who worked there and most of the customers. As he sat there, he checked each visitor with his memory and found that between 11:30 and 1:00, there had been no one who entered who did not have at least a passing acquaintance.

Leaving the bar at 1:00 a.m., he crossed the street, moved a block toward his apartment, and stood in the shelter of a closed grocery store. His check of the cars along his block was slow and easy. One car stood out. The vehicle had been there when he first approached his block. It was still there and had at least two passengers. It was too dark to see the colors or the make of the car, but you could see the flame of a match for a cigarette being lit.

Dave moved down the side street toward the alley. He kept in the shadows to the end of the first garage. He paused there to observe the scene. The alley was dark. With a half-moon above, he could make out some objects. Slowly he crept toward the back of his apartment building. He opened the back door after some thirty seconds of fumbling with his keys. Taking off his shoes, he tiptoed up the back stairway to the third floor. Dave wondered about the hallway light showing through his front windows when he opened his apartment door.

The hallway lights were alternating every five feet along both walls. Dave proceeded down the hallway deftly and, using his handkerchief, unscrewed the lights until his door was cloaked in darkness. It seemed like an eternity as he opened his door just enough to slip through. Once inside, he allowed his eyes to grow accustomed to the dark.

He walked cautiously across the living room and, peering through the drapes, looked through the window at the car parked by the curb. A match was struck inside the car, and the outline of the driver of the surveillance team was visible.

Dave secured the apartment, put his gun under the pillow, lay down on

the bed, and closed his eyes. He would worry about his two visitors in the morning.

Emmett Massey woke Frank up at the break of dawn. Frank was not happy to be woken so rudely at 4:30 a.m. Emmett voiced his consolation and began to make breakfast.

"Well, I can see I won't get any sympathy from you," Frank muttered loud enough to be heard.

"I'm moving you to a friend's cabin, as I am going to be gone a couple of days and I don't want to leave you alone." Emmett looked at his friend and forced a smile.

Frank knew he was being a pest. *God,* he thought, *if I could just get rid of this damn cast and scratch my leg, I wouldn't be so cranky.* "I'm sorry, old buddy."

"Look Frank, I'm going to be in Washington for a couple of days. Immediately after breakfast, I'm going to call my friend at the FBI and see what he can give me on the general I mentioned. Then I'll drop you off at my friend's cabin, drive to Ft. Snelling, and catch a C-130 to Andrews." Massey took a deep breath. "When I show up at the base, someone is going to put this under a microscope and come up with two plus two. When that happens, I don't want you to be here."

"Okay, okay. I'm just giving you a hard time. Besides, I could take care of myself." Frank was still not completely convinced.

"Well, let's eat breakfast so we can get on the road." Massy thought about all the possible things that could happen and felt that his friend's move was necessary in order to keep him safe.

After Frank ate a full breakfast, he helped in every way he could. While he didn't like the move, he understood the necessity. Besides, Massey knew that he would be safe with someone that could not be connected with him.

After seven rings, a woman sleepily answered the phone. "Clements, may I help you?" Her voice was low and sexy, with a southern drawl to it.

Massey recognized Virginia's voice immediately. "Virginia, it's Emmett. You better watch the way you answer the phone. I could have been a stranger."

"Emmett, strangers aren't the people I have to worry about. You want to talk to me or my sleep-deprived husband?"

"Virginia, if I know you, I know why your husband is sleep-deprived. I'd rather chat with you, but give me your lucky mate." Emmett smiled at the thought of Virginia reaching over to wake her husband.

"You know, Emmett, ever since you were my best man some seventeen years ago, you've been trying to make out with my wife—in a nice way, of course. When she brushes you off, you always settle for me. How come?" John Clement was on a roll and was giving his good friend a hard time.

"Well, sweetheart,"—Emmett put on his best imitation of Humphrey Bogart—"you're the only other one available."

"Where are you, good buddy?"

"I'm in Minnesota, but I'll be at Andrews Air Force Base about six this evening and I'd like to visit with you for a couple of hours." Massey did not plan to spend more than three days in DC, as he considered it the armpit of the nation.

"You know you're always welcome. When I tell Virginia, she'll be all excited until you get here." John realized that he had left an opening.

"What happens when I get there?" Massey did not rise to the occasion and waited for what he knew would be another wise remark.

"Cause when you're here, the excitement wears off fast when she realizes how old you are." John could be mean to his best friend.

"I'm not that old, yet. John, I need a favor, and it's serious. In fact, it may be the most serious thing I've ever been mixed up with."

"Sergeant Major, you know all you have to do is ask." John looked at his wife with a questioning look on his face.

"This time it isn't just asking and you doing; it may mean your job is on the line." Massey paused. "I won't ask till I get there, and if you turn me down, I'll understand."

John knew better than to press his old friend. "Okay. I'll pick you up at base-ops when you arrive. See you at six."

"See you at six." Massey hung up the phone, turned, paid the attendant for his gas, and strolled to his pickup truck.

Dave had not slept well the previous night. His perceived tail was still parked outside of his apartment at six in the morning. He left at seven and exited the way he had come in. He walked about three blocks to the bus stop and waited in a doorway until the bus pulled up to the corner. He mounted swiftly behind four other passengers and rode the bus to city hall. The clock on the bell tower gave the time as 7:30.

His arrival at his desk acted like a signal to his lieutenant, who called him immediately to his office. He apprised his immediate supervisor of the progress on the case and advised him that he had proof positive that the bartender at the Hidden Palace Lounge had been lying. As he left the lieutenant's office, he whirled around. "Sir, did you have a tail on me last night or this morning?"

"Hell no!" The lieutenant looked at Brokowski as if he was off his rocker. "Why do you ask?"

"Because there was a car parked in front of my apartment building all night with two men in it. They acted as if they were on a stakeout."

"Dave, let me give the precinct a call and see if our patrols saw them. Maybe they have something on them." The lieutenant looked concerned. "Dave, are you sure you weren't seeing things?"

"No, sir!" With that final remark, Detective David Brokowski returned to his desk and called Ramsey County.

The Ramsey County sheriff's office received the call from the Minneapolis police department at eight in the morning.

Detective Brokowski wanted to know about the body that had been found in a lake last Sunday morning. Since the deceased had been identified as an Air National Guard member, he wanted to know if there was any connection with another Air Guard member who had been found shot to death in Minneapolis last Friday.

The deputy responding to Detective Brokowski's request advised the detective that they had not started an in-depth investigation. What they had discovered was that the man had fallen from a great height and had broken his neck and numerous other parts of his body upon landing. What he fell out of and why, they had no idea. He was dressed in military fatigues with no identification. The fingerprints had been sent to the FBI lab where a positive identification had been made on Tuesday.

"His name was Mike Swanson; he was a member of the Air National Guard and was the wings motor pool sergeant. He didn't come home on Saturday night, and he was reported missing early Sunday morning by his wife." The deputy went on, "Why don't you come over? We'll show you what else we've got."

Dave Brokowski thought for just a few seconds. "Thanks. I'll be there about one."

Sergeant Major Emmett Massey arrived at the Air Reserve Base Operations at 10:00 a.m. A C-130 was being towed out of the hanger and appeared to be the aircraft that would carry him to Andrews.

Checking in to Base Operations in civilian clothes was common practice for retired members of the armed services. Emmett pulled out his ID card and was immediately recognized as a rare breed. The sergeant major in the rank box was enough to insure some special attention.

Major James Forestall, no relation to the famous wartime secretary, welcomed the sergeant major and four other retired members to his aircraft. "Listen up. Our freight today is electronic gear needed at Andrews. We will be landing at Wright-Patterson to take on two more crates. At Wright-Pat, we will stand down for about two hours for lunch. At about 1630, we will depart Wright-

Patterson and touch down at Andrews at about 1800. They will remain overnight at Andrews for three nights departing at 1300 on Sunday. Do you have any questions?"

That question was asked as a matter of courtesy, and no one responded as the major simply turned around and joined the copilot and the navigator.

With the flight plan announced, the passengers bordered the aircraft and took their seats on either side of the aircraft facing the freight.

The call to the National Guard in St. Paul, Minnesota, came at 10:45 in the morning. There seemed to be a sheriff from Wisconsin on the line who wanted to report a strange situation that had occurred the night before.

Sergeant Major John Jameston picked up the phone. "Sergeant Major Jameston, may I help you?'

"Sheriff Muncie from Polk County, Wisconsin. We're near the Wisconsin-Minnesota border and would like to report what appears to be a theft of military equipment,"

"Okay. What type of military equipment?" The sergeant major asked his question in a bored manner, as he thought this theft was about some obsolete typewriters. *Boy,* he thought, *this has got to be my worst day.*

"Look,"—the sheriff sounded a little pissed off—"for your information there is a whole barn and a farmhouse full of equipment. Most of it's electronic gear, but there are two generators and weapons."

With that, the sergeant major signaled his commanding officer to pick up his phone.

"Sheriff, this is Major Francis. Would you repeat what you just said to the sergeant major?"

"Major Francis, I don't have time to repeat my statements. But I will say that someone is missing a few M-16 rifles. Now, do you have some more questions, or would you rather come over and find out what's going on?"

At the mention of weapons, Francis was about to say, "Call AFT," but he thought better of it. "Sergeant Major Jameston and I will be over as soon as possible. Where are you located, sheriff?"

"Take US 8 East, out of Minnesota for about nine miles, turn left on State 46 for about two, maybe three miles, and you'll find us in Balsam Lake. It's Polk County seat, and any gas station can give you directions. My office is in the county building, first floor."

Before Major Francis could ask for more information, the sheriff hung up.

The deputy was smiling broadly at the sheriff. "Boss, you made it sound as though we had found a whole armory instead of only two M-16s."

"Hey, they didn't ask, and I didn't volunteer. I also didn't tell them that the farm is owned by an Air National Guard officer from Minnesota." The sheriff smiled back. "Let them find out for themselves."

CHAPTER FOURTEEN

At 2:00 p.m. on Thursday afternoon, two gentlemen dressed in Army uniforms walked into the Polk County Courthouse. Major Francis, the younger of the two, appeared to be there more as an observer than the higher ranking individual. Sergeant Major Jameston, the older of the two, appeared to have much more experience.

Sheriff Muncie looked up from his desk and smiled. He took the identification of the sergeant major and studied it with great interest. "I've never seen such a beautiful ID in my life." He grinned like a country bumpkin, as he handed it back to the sergeant major.

Major Francis looked around the room and thought, *Boy, this has got to be out of the nineteenth century.* Looking at the roll-top desk, he wondered just how old the furniture was.

"If you like the desk, sonny, you can have it for about five… if I decide to sell it." The sheriff looked at the young officer and decided to play the dummy for a little longer.

"Sheriff, I'm Major Francis, and this is Sergeant Major Jameston." Francis looked directly into the eyes of the sheriff. "What's this about stolen government property and weapons?"

"Well, you see, it's a long story, so why don't both of you sit down and take a load off your feet? Out here, we don't rush so much."

"Thanks sheriff." *I don't think this sheriff is as dumb as he sounds. In fact, I think he may be smarter than both of us and definitely more experienced.*

"We got a call from two fishermen who—let me say this properly, so as not to get my fishermen friends in trouble—stumbled across a barn which was left open. In that barn, there were stacks and stacks of military equipment. Included in that batch, and we are talking more than one batch, were two M16s."

"You keep mentioning batches. Just what does a 'batch' mean?" Francis guessed that the sheriff was purposely trying to drag the meeting out as long as possible.

"The equipment and weapons are out at the old Spalding farm. When we say 'batches,' we're talking about the barn, three floors in the farmhouse, and the cellar." The sheriff looked first at Francis and then at Jameston.

"Where is this place?" Francis's voice was hard in a no-nonsense way.

"About ten miles from here, but you will need excellent directions, or you can follow us." The sheriff picked up his hat, motioned to his deputy, and strolled from the room.

The blacktop road marked "Polk County 14" going out of town had been good for about five miles. It was the turn on the gravel road that roughed up the two airmen. The meandering trail proved to be unsafe in places, and one had to maneuver around holes and lumps. At times the road almost touched the lakes that it handily curved around.

Suddenly the sheriff's pickup truck stopped. Ahead of his vehicle a tow truck partially blocked the road. There were three men standing next to another pickup. It was obvious that the tow was about to pull the Ford pickup into town. Two of the men waved at the sheriff and began to chat. The guardsmen's car came to a complete stop as they waited for the sheriff to complete his conversation.

Major Francis opened the passenger's door and climbed out. He walked slowly over to the group of men conversing quietly in the center of the road. "Hi, sheriff. May I interrupt?"

"Sure, major. These are the two fishermen I told you about. They were just getting ready to go into town with the tow truck driver."

Francis looked at the two and decided to get their addresses from the sheriff. "Have you got their addresses?"

The sheriff smiled. "You bet."

"Great. How much further to the site?"

"Well, major, if you look out across that field, you can just make out the back of a barn. That's it, and the house is over the rise in front of the barn." The sheriff pointed toward the group of buildings about a half mile away.

Turning toward the two fishermen, Major Francis smiled. "Gentlemen, you'll be in town for a few hours, won't you?" Without waiting for an answer, he continued, "We may want to ask you a few questions for our report."

"Sure, major. I can't leave till tomorrow, so we'll be at the Bed Time Motel. It's on the edge of town."

The major nodded and returned to his car. "I'm sure glad our car didn't hit that rock. It would have totaled it." Sergeant Major Jameston agreed and began to edge the car around the rocks and the tow truck.

Once again the guardsmen followed the sheriff along the gravel road. Every so often, the trees seemed to hide every thing in sight, bringing much-needed shade and a cooling of the air. The sheriff turned on a blacktop county road and spurted about a half mile to a white clapboard farmhouse of the 1880's vintage. He turned his pickup truck abruptly into a beautifully kept gravel drive and slid to a stop in the side yard of the house.

The guardsmen looked surprised at the tarred, two-lane county road. Posted on the side of the road, just as the car turned, was the county identification, "Polk County 14." It was obvious to the guardsmen that the sheriff had taken them out of the way, over a treacherous, rough trail someone had comically called a road.

Climbing out of the vehicle, the sergeant major showed his temper. He yelled, "Really sheriff, how far is thisfarm from town?"

"Oh, the way we came, it's about thirteen miles; by blacktop county road, it's about eight miles." He grinned at the slight smile on the major's face. "I just thought you guys would like a tour of our backcountry, and I had to check on the tow truck and the two fishermen."

"Sheriff, I don't like being fooled." Jameston's temper flared even higher. "We could have been here about fifteen minutes ago!"

"No, Sergeant Major Jameston, you could have been here almost a half hour ago." The sheriff turned and walked up the path toward the house. "Let's show you what we found. By the way, I have a search warrant."

Stepping into the house, the guardsmen were surprised by the quality of the nineteenth century furniture. The first three rooms were filled with beautifully kept antiques. It was the second floor plus the attic and the cellar that intrigued the guardsmen.

"Have you seen enough?" The sheriff had been watching the two guardsmen as they wrote in their notebooks.

"For the house, yes. Let's go out to the barn." Major Francis noticed the lack of weapons and wondered why the sheriff had mentioned that there was a weapons cache. "Sheriff, where are the weapons you mentioned on the phone?"

There are two M16s in the closet of the office and a .45 pistol in the desk drawer. "Oh, I forgot to show you the office." The sheriff almost sounded apologetic.

"Well, let's see it. I'll get some serial numbers off the weapons, if you don't mind."

Francis was beginning to get upset at having to play twenty questions every time he needed something.

"Sure, Major Francis. Anything you want." The sheriff motioned toward a double sliding door off the first floor hallway.

Inside the dining-room-turned-office, Major Francis noticed an appointment book and an address book on either side of the phone. Major Francis opened the drawers to the desk to look inside. The center drawer had been forced open. He was surprised that the rest of the drawers were unlocked. The .45 was in the top right-hand drawer. He turned around, decided to open the closet doors, and found the two M16s. He read off the serial numbers of the three weapons as Sergeant Major Jameston wrote them down.

Major Francis turned back to the desk and picked up the address book and paged through it. He turned to Jameston. "Make a few photo copies of some of the pages. I want to see about a few numbers. Sheriff, if you don't mind, we would like to talk to some of the people in this book. I want to see about a few members of this business, especially First Communications Incorporated." He had used the name of the corporation that he found in the book. The four men left the house and moved toward the barn.

"Hold on to your hats," quipped the sheriff, as he threw open the doors of the barn. It was the sergeant major who was the first to speak. "My god! You could supply an army with what's in this barn."

"No." Francis was being his realistic self. "You could supply a good-sized unit."

The two Army guardsmen and the sheriff moved inside the barn. Jameston began to take down serial numbers from the equipment. It would be three more hours before the group would complete the inventory and leave the barn.

Sergeant Major Emmett Massey stepped off the C130 and immediately headed across the ramp toward Base Operations. The evening was hot and muggy, with a smell of rain in the air. As he approached Operations, he spotted his friend waving to him. He smiled as he quickened his pace.

John Clement took Massey's bag and entered the building. Massey, following, stepped inside just as the rain began to fall. The time was 1810, military time.

"Virginia's waiting in the car." John smiled as he and Emmett passed through base-ops and headed for the parking lot.

"Great. Let me take you out to dinner. We'll go over to the NCO club and get a steak and maybe a glass of beer. How's that, good buddy?"

"Sounds great to me, Emmett." With that, John opened the outside door and both began to run toward the parking lot.

Before they had gone five steps, a blue Chrysler Newport braked to a stop in front of them. Virginia leaned over and unlocked the passenger door. John quickly jumped into the front seat and unlocked the back door in almost the same motion.

Emmett threw his one bag into the back seat and climbed in after it. The car pulled off as John told his wife to head for the NCO club. Virginia looked upset. "I think I'd rather head for home. This looks like an all-night rain. I'll put some steaks on and fry up some French fries. John, you open three bottles of beer, and we'll settle down for the evening."

"Hell, Virginia, that sounds like a great idea. I'll do the dishes when we're done." Massey looked at Virginia, winked, and smiled broadly.

The steak at John Clements's house was superb. The French fried potatoes were golden brown and delicious. The carrots and peas were fresh and tender. With the meal finished, Virginia cleared the dishes while Emmett washed and John dried. With the work done, the three began to reminisce. Sitting at the table, the three spoke quietly while they sipped a second ice-cold beer.

Virginia, sensing the need for the men to be alone, excused herself to go freshen up. "Well, don't take too long—we may need your advice." Her husband glanced at Emmett and smiled. "Okay buddy, what's the big, deep, dark secret?"

With Virginia receding toward the other end of the dining room, Emmett spoke softly yet clearly. "I've got a murder, a kidnapping, a theft of government property, and fraud."

"You've got to be kidding, Emmett." John leaned closer to Emmett's face and studied his eyes. "My god, you're not kidding."

"Never been more serious in my life." Emmett was just beginning to say more when John motioned him to be quiet.

"Emmett, let's go for a walk. It will be good for our digestion." He paused as he watched his wife approach from across the dining room. "You can tell me all about it, and I'll see what we can do."

John looked at his wife and then at Emmett. He could never understand how his wife and Emmett could read each other like a book. "Sorry, Virginia. Emmett and I have some serious business to talk about tonight. Maybe we can all go for a walk tomorrow."

The serious look on John's face silenced the light retort that Virginia was about to make. The two set off on their walk with umbrellas raised, looking like a modern-day Holmes and Watson. At least, that's what Virginia thought as she watched them slowly disappear.

Major Francis and Sergeant Major Jameston sat with Sheriff Muncie and talked seriously about the ownership of both the farm and the corporation. Major Peter Spaulding was the owner of the farm. From the paperwork found by the sheriff, the corporation was formed in Minnesota during 1954. Its stock ownership was unknown, but its corporate attorneys were listed as Feeny, Gabrielson, Mathews, and Peters.

Peter Spaulding was the commander of the 1327th Air Traffic Control Flight. As the commander of the unit, he was also head of the state MARS program.

Spaulding had been in charge of the program since assuming command in 1960. Before that, he had served as the unit supply officer. While the supply officer, he was an attorney in the same law office that formed the corporation. The attorney had been commander from 1953 until 1960, when the unit received its federal recognition as an air traffic control unit.

There was a difference in the command of the unit. All National Guard units have a full-time staff. They are called "technicians. While the attorney was commander, the unit supply officer was full-time. When Spaulding assumed command, the full-time technician slot had been moved to the commander's slot. Consequently, the length of time that the theft was going could dictate just how deep and, possibly, just how high the corruption went.

The two guardsmen wrapped up their discussion with the sheriff and the two fishermen who had first discovered the equipment. They requested the address book and the weapons, which had been retrieved from the farm by now, signed a hand receipt for the weapons, made copies of all the paperwork, including the address book, and departed at 9:00 p.m.

The sheriff was glad to be relieved of the case. Military property was involved,

making it a federal problem and besides, it looked like a "hot potato." Watching the two guardsmen get in their car, the sheriff breathed a sigh of relief. "Have a good trip back to St. Paul," yelled the sheriff. "Oh, and if you ever want to leave your jobs, give me a call. I can always use a couple of deputies."

"Thanks sheriff," Major Francis yelled back. "You may be seeing us sooner than you think."

"I expect I will," the sheriff yelled back. Turning to his deputy, he murmured, "I feel sorry for those poor guys."

"Why did you say that, sheriff?" The deputy had not caught the seriousness of the situation.

"Because this thing could step on a lot of powerful toes, and I would not want to be in those guardsmen's shoes for anything." The look on the sheriff's face told the deputy to figure the rest out for himself.

CHAPTER FIFTEEN

Sergeant Major Massey waited patiently as his friend worked the telephone at his desk in the FBI building in Washington, DC. He was on the fifth call when he hung up and looked at the sergeant. "Your general friend is retired, and no one seems to know anything about him. In fact, I can't even get a telephone number for him."

"That's strange. Of course, I haven't seen him in some five years." Massey wondered just what the general was involved in to make him that invisible.

"Let me make one more phone call to our Minneapolis office. Maybe they've got something on the unit or the commander that you've told me about." He waited now for Emmett to respond.

"John, if you call Minneapolis, we don't know just who is going to find out about the inquiry. Maybe I'm paranoid, but do you know anybody in Minneapolis that will be discreet?"

Just then the telephone rang. "Clement." The short response was typical of John Clement when he was upset and something disturbed him in his thinking process.

"This is Major Francis in Minneapolis, Agent Clement. I'm looking for a retired Sergeant Major Massey."

"Major Francis, what unit do you belong to, and why did you call me?"

"Agent Clement, I'm a technician in the Minnesota Army National Guard. The sergeant major and I have been assigned by the general to find out what is going on with the 1327th Air Traffic Control Flight and the commander and the unauthorized sale of military equipment."

"Major, is that case dealing with a major named Peter Spaulding?"

"How did you know?" Francis was surprised that an FBI agent would already know about the case when he didn't know about the thefts until yesterday afternoon.

"I've got a friend who flew in last night from Minnesota. This friend of mine told me about a Major Peter Spaulding and the 1327th Air Traffic Control Flight. It seems that there has been at least one death and possibly one more in connection with that problem." John paused to allow the new information to sink into Major Francis's head. "If I were you, I would contact one Thomas J. Mullin, who is the first sergeant of the unit. He's a good guy and should be a lot of help. Now what have you got?"

"Okay. Thanks for the information. We have paperwork on a Minnesota corporation formed by a law firm where the former commander of the unit is a partner. Now that's not enough to pin the attorney if he's innocent of the theft, but we're not sure yet."

"That's not enough for murder. Do you think there is something else besides the theft?"

There was a long pause on the telephone as Francis thought over the question. "It would be enough if the theft was more widespread and involved more than theft of equipment."

"Sergeant Major Massey is with me right now. Why don't you talk to him?" Smiling, Clements began to pass the phone to the sergeant major but suddenly stopped short. "Excuse me...

before you talk to the sergeant major, what's the name of the law firm that set up that corporation?"

"Feeny, Gabrielson, Mathews, and Peters. Now let me talk to the sergeant major."

"Before you do, let me warn you to proceed carefully and be extremely diplomatic with this firm. They're one of the most prestigious in Washington and in Minnesota, if not the nation. If the former commander is involved, it could be a political nightmare. Here's the sergeant major now."

"Sergeant Major, I'm Major Francis of the Minnesota Army Nation Guard, and we are interested in any information you can give us on the 1327th Air Traffic Control Flight. I also understand that you are friends with one of their full-time technicians, Frank Valencio. We were wondering if you have any information about his whereabouts."

"Why do you ask? And how did you know I was here?" The sergeant major was overly concerned.

"Sergeant Major, we are friends of Frank's and we are worried about his whereabouts. If you can assure us he's okay, we'll wait till you get back to ask some questions about some equipment that was found on the Spaulding farm in Wisconsin."

"Major, I assure you, he's okay. You don't need to worry about him. How did you know him?"

"Well, we met at a detachment party, but it's a long time ago. In any case, call my house when you get in. Frank knows the number. Okay?"

"By the way, we think the law firm I gave you is heavily involved. You might check them out. See you when you get back."

Massey hung up the phone and looked questioningly at Emmett.

Emmett looked at Massey and explained, " The law firm of Feeny, Gabrielson, Mathews, and Peters is the law firm that set up a corporation for Spaulding. I know they are connected to the CIA . . . how, I'm not sure."

Massey glanced at Emmett and wondered out loud, "The CIA is not supposed to be operating in the United States. Isn't that the FBI's bailiwick?"

"Sure. But with those cowboys, anything is possible." Clements stopped for a second before proceeding. "I think the agency is much more active stateside than what is commonly believed."

Dave Brokowsky had just signed in when the telephone on his desk began to ring. Since this was Friday, he hoped he could get away a little early. Tomorrow was the beginning of his weekend UTA, and he could use the extra time to complete a military home study course he was taking. "Homicide, Detective Brokowski."

The voice on the other end could only have been Brian Donnley's.

"Brian, I'm glad you called. The Minnesota Guard is involved somehow. I'm meeting with a Major Francis and a Sergeant Major Jameston in about a half hour. Have you got anything else that I should know?"

"How the hell did they get involved?" Brian was completely upset over this new wrinkle.

"I don't know yet, but I've got a suspicion that it has something to do with the military. What do you think?" Dave twisted a knob on the radio as he waited for a response.

"Dave, I think I might have something that matches. Mullins told me about a farm in Wisconsin. Apparently he's been moving some of the equipment out to that farm for a while. If that's true, he's guilty of interstate transportation of stolen goods. Add that to the fact that it's military equipment, and you have a federal case."

"When did you get that information?" Dave was beginning to think that Brian had been holding out on him.

Major Peter Spaulding finished his meeting with the non-commissioned officers and advised them on the times he expected to follow when the middle weekend started. It was the middle weekend period that all those serving during the two-week summer field training looked forward to. This weekend period fell seven days after the beginning of the period, or midway. The troops were supposed to be off from Saturday at noon to Sunday evening. In reality some of the troops stretched this from Friday evening at about 2:30 p.m., until almost midnight Sunday night.

In a mobile air traffic control unit, various sections would provide services all through the middle of the weekend. In the 1327th some of the senior non-commissioned officers would pull shift in tower, GCA, maintenance, motor pool, and the orderly room to ensure the proper manning of these facilities. By pulling shift, these NCOs could allow their lower ranking men to take full advantage of the time off.

First Sergeant Thomas J. Mullins remained during this middle weekend to insure a command presence. The clerk, Thomas William Trent, would be released for the weekend at 4:40 p.m. Friday afternoon and not have to sign in until Sunday at 5:00 p. m. The major would depart on Friday evening and would return Monday at 7:00 a.m.

Major Peter Spaulding pulled through the main gate at 7:00 p.m. on the way to a restaurant west of St.Cloud. While the dinner would be partially business, it would be a nice, relaxing preamble to a long weekend away from the military.

The restaurant and bar had been built in 1936, out of whole logs. This building had been extensively remodeled in 1949 and redecorated in 1960. The steps leading to a wide porch led directly to the front entrance. The porch, which was open, ran the entire length of the log structure and wrapped around the right side to allow passage to a rear porch that fronted on the water. A second set of steps of about six feet in width ran from the side porch to a walkway that led to the parking lot.

Peter and his acquaintance sat at the bar and exchanged what appeared to be pleasantries. Whenever a waitress, the bartender, or the busboy approached, they appeared to switch subjects and continued to speak in quiet tones. Not even the couple next to them could make out just what was being said.

Both ordered a second drink, and thirty minutes later, when their table was ready, they entered the dining room with two fresh drinks. Their table overlooked the back porch, and they had a beautiful view of the lake. The time now was 9:00 p.m., and the water glistened with the sinking sun.

Tom Mullins left the camp at 2100 military time and drove to Little Falls. There he stopped at a gas station that had a pay phone. He dialed the resort's number in Merrifield. It was almost ten minutes before Brian Donnley picked up the phone.

"God, what took you so long, Detective?"

Brian, on his part, had rushed as fast as he could once the owner of the establishment had found him on the dock. He had protested at first at the imposition upon his and his wife's quiet time. They had felt like teenagers as they waited for the rising moon to appear in the mirror-like surface of the calm waters. He had not wanted to go, but his wife urged him on with the assurance that she would wait at this very spot for her lover's return.

"Sergeant, you pick the worst time to call. Don't you have any feelings for a man on vacation with his family?"

"Detective, I'm terribly sorry, but I thought your children would like to attend the parade tomorrow morning. It happens at 0800 and should take about forty-five minutes. I can show your family around the base, and we can have lunch at the NCO club. How's that?"

"Perfect, Mr. Donnley. See you at 7:30 tomorrow morning." The first sergeant hung up and headed for his friend's house near downtown Little Falls.

Brian smiled. The first sergeant was apparently afraid that his conversation would be overheard. Since he knew that the detective understood the military mentality, he also understood that any "request" by a superior officer was the same as an order. Putting two and two together, he would meet the first sergeant and discuss whatever information he had.

Major Spaulding's dinner mate was a tall man of approximately six feet two inches. In that frame, he carried a muscular 180 pounds and wore a short, military-style haircut for his dark brown hair. His face reflected a hardened experience which could only have been obtained after many years of warrior-type effort.

When the waitress asked for their orders, the muscular man ordered two steak and lobster dinners, two more drinks to be served before dinner, and a bottle of the restaurant's finest chardonnay to be served with dinner. It was after the meal that Major Spaulding complained about being sick.

"Miss!" the warrior-type called out to the waitress. "My friend is not feeling well. If you don't mind, bring us the bill."

The waitress realized that the man's friend was getting progressively worse. Both men got to their feet and, with his friend's help, Peter Spaulding was slowly escorted to the door to the back porch. "Boy, am I sick." Peter staggered slightly.

"It's okay, major. You probably need some air. Let's take a walk out to the end of the dock. The fresh air will do you good." Peter allowed himself to be helped.

His orders were simple: "Keep Major Peter Spaulding from saying too much when the Air Guard, detectives, or the FBI come calling." That he sometimes went too far in carrying out such orders was also understood by his immediate supervisors.

Peter Spaulding reached the end of the dock only by the help of his friend. Reaching the far end, his body felt immobile. He stood looking out at the lake, but for some strange reason, he did not feel a thing. It was as though he was paralyzed. Instinctively, he attempted to talk, only to find nothing came out. He felt his body being pushed toward the edge of the dock, and although he attempted to push back, he felt his body falling forward. He attempted to turn just as his face and body hit the water in unison.

Peter Spaulding's mind told him to fight, but his body moved ever so slowly. He took one last deep breath just before he began to sink into the lake's dark enclosure.

CHAPTER SIXTEEN

The two old men carefully maneuvered their boat through the weed beds that lined the shore of the small bay that they often fished. They slowly trolled just off the shore where a restaurant sat overlooking the water. It was four in the morning, and the only light that could be seen from their boat was the one at the end of the dock. Suddenly the line began to sing as the hook dug deep into something in the water.

With a jerk, the older of the two fishermen set the hook more deeply and began to play his line. Something was wrong, the old man thought. The line just didn't feel right. He looked at his partner and shouted to cut the engine. This done, the old man slowly began to real in his sixteen-pound test line. The Garcia fishing rod bent nearly double as the boat began to be pulled back toward an object that was barely visible floating in the water.

"Hey, Joe." The older of the two fishermen spoke to his friend of thirty years for the first time since he had gotten his line caught in the water. "This isn't caught in a weed bed. It looks like it's caught some clothes, and they're pretty heavy."

Joe slowly began to row toward the area where his friend's line was caught. As he pulled the fourteen-foot fishing boat closer, both men began to make out the shape. "Looks like a body." Joe crossed himself and continued to edge the boat closer to the object.

The two men secured the body to the side of the boat and restarted the engine, slowly moving to the end of the restaurant's dock. Tying the boat securely to the end of the dock, Joe moved toward the restaurant, hoping to find a phone. The body of Major Peter Spaulding had been in the water a little more than five hours.

Dave Brokowsky looked at his reflection in the mirror and finished shaving. He stepped into the kitchen and poured himself a cup of coffee. He took a seat at his table and began to go over his notes for the forth time. The meeting with the two air guardsmen had gone well. He had learned as much from the airmen as they had learned from him.

He entered the bedroom of his apartment and put on his class-A uniform. His appearance in the hallway's full-length mirror reflected a captain in the United States Army. He picked up his hat, placed it firmly on his head, exited the front door, and walked to his car. He had a thirty-minute drive to Fort Snelling.

The drive to the base was uneventful. He passed through the main gate at 7:25 a.m. The guard on the gate snapped to attention and saluted. Dave, returning the salute, thought about the tradition. In the modern world, saluting while driving an automobile through a gate in traffic was foolish. Oh well. Tradition dies slowly in the military. Maybe it would change in thirty or forty years.

The clapboard buildings on the base were relics of World War II. They had been built during the forties as temporary structures.

The buildings, better than almost thirty years later, were still in fairly good condition. He passed the base chapel also built with clapboards—a replicated design model as a thousand other base chapels around the country.

He passed the flight line on his right side with most of the base buildings on his left. He proceeded through the guard side and entered the original Fort Snelling. On his right side was a golf course. Reaching the road to the east of the golf course, he turned right and drove between the course and the old polo grounds. He directed his vehicle toward the row of nineteenth century, brick, three-story buildings on the south side of the fort.

He turned his vehicle into the parking lot that was used for the intelligence unit. Parking his car in a spot reserved for officers, he moved quickly up the front stairs and proceeded to his office on the second floor. The time was 7:30 a.m.

Retired Sergeant Major Emmett Massey finished his morning coffee and began to pace back and forth on the deck of his friend's home. Virginia was in the kitchen preparing her famous omelets. Her breakfast on a Saturday was more like a brunch, and anyone delving into the meal would not even think of eating until six or seven that evening. John was out running as he prepared for a busy Saturday.

Massey thought about his up-and-coming meeting with the ex-spook from the CIA. From what John Clements had told him, the guy had never steered John wrong in the twenty years that they had known each other. More importantly, the ex-spook had left the active part of the agency and now held a position with the inspector general's office. If there was a rouge group working within the CIA, that agency would be the one to filter it out. At least that was the idea.

It was roughly ten minutes after he had left that John Clement came running up the drive. "You look like an old man, John." Massey's wisecrack after he watched his friend winding down was meant more as praise. After all, Emmett had not run a mile for…oh, maybe all of four years.

"Sure, Emmett. And I suppose you could walk the mile faster than I could run it."

"Now you got it, buddy."

Virginia looked at these two lifelong friends and saw the little boys still were coming out at each remark. "Okay, heroes. John, get your shower before I put out the breakfast, and make it snappy. I'm getting hungry."

The ringing of the phone caused all of them to jump. John reached across the table and picked it up. "The Clement's," John's face suddenly turned an ashen white. He glanced at Massey and shook his head from side to side. His only conversation was a short "Thank you." His hand shook slightly as he carefully hung up the phone.

"Our meeting is off." John's voice was hard with a tinge of dread. "He's been ordered to head up a team of investigators on the way to Nam." He paused before continuing. "He leaves this afternoon. The orders came from the inspector general."

Massey looked apprehensively at both of the Clements. His first words were chosen carefully as he began to discuss the obvious. "This may be a method of cutting off our direct connection with the CIA. What is your make on this, John?"

"I'm not sure, but this friend of mine said he would do a little checking first. I hope that checking wasn't the cause of his orders." John looked at Emmett. "Well, just maybe I can find out something at the office."

Brian Donnley drove his car through the stone gates of Fort Ripley at 7:30 a.m. Just inside the fort, Senior Master Sergeant Mullins waited patiently in his military pickup truck. He noticed Donnley and his family as they passed through the main gate.

Tooting his horn, he pulled out of the parking area and swung around Donnley's passenger car. Waving furiously, he proceeded north on the main road toward the reviewing stand, immediately followed by Donnley. The pickup truck slowly proceeded to just past the reviewing stand where Mullins pulled into a parking lot. Donnley followed.

The site had been previously picked and arranged by Mullins. It was in front of a friend's orderly room, one that had a high-speed copy machine. During Friday night the lights had burned most the night, and if you stopped to listen, the copy machine had worked the same length of time.

Thc vehicles were parked on the back side of the building, which kept them unseen from the street. If one stood across the street from the front side of the building, it was the perfect place to review the parade.

The reviewing stand stood on the east side of the parade grounds that stretched away toward the governor's mansion. In the middle of the parade ground was a tiny air strip with two sod runways. The airfield buildings were located at the far north end of the field. At this distance, you could make out three trailer-like structures that were foreign to the field. They were spread out along the runways. These were the mobile units of the 1327th Air Traffic Control Flight.

The parade at Camp Ripley was a strictly military affair. The troops were marched in individual units to their pre-selected sites on the side farther from and facing the reviewing stand. As in all military formations, the troops arrived early enough so that an intervening few minutes were needed before the parade began.

In this case, they arrived just about the time that Mullins pulled through the main gate.

Lucky for Mullins and Donnley, they had pulled into the parking lot just before a company of troops blocked the road leading to the site that Mullins had so carefully picked out. While the children and Helen moved toward the front of the building, Mullins and Donnley began the task of moving files from the buildings to their respective cars. That accomplished, the two joined Donnley's family to view the parade.

At 8:45 the awards and the parade ceremony came to an end. The marching men moved toward their encampments while Mullins led the Donnleys back to their vehicles.

"Tom, where do we go from here?" Brian smiled as he watched his son tell his sister and mother about the parade that they had seen.

"Brian, follow me. I'm going to stop by my orderly room for a moment, and then we'll go over to the NCO club for brunch."

Tom Mullins pulled his truck out of the parking lot with Brian following in his car. It took only five minutes for the two vehicles to park side by side at the units' parking lot. Corrugated tent structures built on concrete pads lined both sides of the unit area.

Entering the orderly room, the sergeant flipped on a radio, and the sounds of Glen Miller came booming out.

"Now that I have a copy of the files, I have some information for you. Major Spaulding's farm was raided by the headquarters of the Minnesota National Guard."

Sergeant Thomas Mullins looked surprised. "Hum. That's strange. If I remember right, the farm is pretty much out of the way."

"Yes. Some fishermen tried to take shelter in the barn and discovered all kinds of military equipment. They got suspicious and called the sheriff. The sheriff took one look and called the Minnesota National Guard." Brian unconsciously studied the face of the sergeant as he relayed the information. "I don't know if this is connected to the Bascom murder and Valencio's disappearance, but it may just tie together."

At the mention of Frank Valencio's name, Tom Mullins leaned over to Brian and whispered, "Frank isn't missing. He's recuperating from a broken leg. He's in a safe place."

A look of disbelief appeared in Brian's eyes before he answered in kind. "Mullins, what else are you holding back on me?"

"That's it. Besides, I didn't find out about this until after the last time we personally talked. Under the circumstances, I did not want to mention it on the phone.

"What circumstances?" Brian was beginning to speak louder than a whisper.

"Keep it down, Detective. I think the provost marshal has a tap on us." Tom Mullins held a finger to his lips and continued to whisper. "Frank's a witness to another murder and we think he's in danger."

"Sarge, as the officers and NCOs used to tell me, leave the thinking to us." He smiled at the look on Mullins's face.

The ring of the telephone interrupted their conversation. "1327th Orderly room, First Sergeant Mullins."

"First Sergeant, this is the provost marshal's office. Report to my office ASAP." He added, almost like an afterthought, "Oh, and bring Detective Donnley with you."

"Yes, sir. It'll take a few minutes; I have to get someone to relieve me." Tom put the phone on the cradle and looked puzzled.

"We're going to have to put that brunch off for a while. We have to report to the provost marshal's office as soon as possible."

Brian was disturbed by Mullins's facial features. The frown and the distinguishing look of puzzlement bothered him. "Did he say why?"

"No. It could be a serious accident or possibly an injury to one of my men."

He smiled. "Or an altercation in town with the foot soldiers."

"Sure...but why me?" Brian looked quizzically at Mullins. "I think we're going to find out something about my case."

Tom Mullins sat there quietly as he contemplated the provost marshal's call for almost a full three minutes before he responded to Brian's statement. "Relief is on the way!"

At precisely 0900, a sergeant entered the orderly room. The sergeant had the appearance of an Irish boxer whose face had been used over and over again as a punching bag. A scar ran the length of his right check, and an old wound was visible on the left side of his neck.

"Brian, meet Master Sergeant James Murphy. He's one of our enlisted Irish Mafia." Turning to Murphy, Tom slowly told him to hold the fort until he returned. "If I'm needed, I'll be at the provost marshal's office and then at the NCO club for brunch."

Spotting Donnley's wife and children, Tom Mullins smiled and moved through the door. "Let's all go back to my truck; it'll give your boy a thrill and something to brag about to his friends." Mullins turned toward Murphy. "Murphy, keep a watch on that car out there in front. If anyone starts to fool around with it, take the .45 out of the drawer and find out what they want. I don't want it touched except by Mr. Donnley."

Murphy smiled broadly. "Consider it as safe as a baby in its mother's arms."

Three sheriffs' cars, plus a state patrol vehicle parked in the restaurant parking lot, reflected the interest in the drowning that had occurred. It was known that the man was one Peter Spaulding. He was in the Air National Guard and he lived in an apartment in St. Paul. There were extremely wet pictures of what appeared to be his family spread out across a table in the restaurant.

The owner had complained loudly when the sheriff had woke him up at 5:30 a.m. and asked him to open the place up. He had calmed down when he heard there had been a drowning off his dock. He had complained even louder when the sheriff requested that all workers who worked last night be called to the restaurant at 8:00 a.m. The complaint fell on deaf ears, and the restaurant now had a full complement of workers sitting around, drinking coffee, and waiting to be called for an interview with the sheriff.

The young blonde waitress and the tall, thin, dark-haired bartender were the only ones that the sheriff asked to stay. By 9:00 a.m., all except those two were on their way home.

"All right, young lady. Tell me about the two men you waited on last night." The sheriff occupied the executive swivel chair in the owner's office.

"Well, they had steak and lobster and about two drinks before dinner, plus wine during the dinner and two more drinks after dinner. That's when the nice gentleman got sick and had to get some air."

"Miss, Judy is your name, isn't it? You said 'nice gentleman.' Was that the victim?"

"Yes, sir."

"What was the other one like? And what did he look like?" The sheriff liked this young girl. She was bright, extremely attractive, and intelligent. She seemed to be sharp enough to pay attention to little things.

"He was good looking…dark complexion…about six foot two. He had a scar on his right cheek and was muscular and about one hundred and eighty pounds. He had a military bearing to him, and so I took him to be military, the same as the other guy."

The sheriff smiled. "Okay. What happened when the other one got sick?"

"The young, good-looking one helped the other one out to the porch and the deck. I got busy about then." Judy was struggling to find just the right words. "I never saw the nice man again, but I saw the other one as he left the porch by the parking lot entrance."

"Judy, you can go home now. Leave your telephone number with the deputy so we can contact you later." Judy rose, and as she started to leave, the sheriff yelled after her, "If you think of anything else, call me. Here's my card. Tell Sam to come in now." Judy smiled, took the card, and left the office.

"Okay Sam, have a seat. You were on duty last night. Do you remember the two men who Judy waited on?"

"Sure, sheriff. They came in about seven and had about three drinks before their table was ready. We were extremely busy, but I don't get many people at the bar. Most arc here for dinner."

"Did you hear them say anything that would give us an idea of how they got along?"

"Sheriff, I make it a strict rule not to listen in on my customers."

"Sure. But just this once, Sam, why don't you break the rules and let me know what you heard?"

"They talked real quiet and seemed to change the subject every time they thought I was getting too close. Well, Spaulding, he mentioned the traffic out the main gate at Ripley. So I think he must be up there for training."

Sam stopped and began to drum his fingers. "The other guy, the one with the scar, seemed to be highly interested in something that the Spaulding guy was holding for him. He called it 'white gold.' But I don't think it was the real item they were talking about."

"'White gold'?" The sheriff looked stumped. "Anything else?"
Sam shook his head slowly. "No. I don't think so."

The provost marshal looked at the two men sitting across his desk. He had seen the Minneapolis detective in the company of Mullins at the parade. The telephone call had come into his office just after the parade, and he had called the 1327th immediately. The Air Guard headquarters wanted to talk to Major Spaulding about his farm. Since the unit commander was not there, it was only normal to call the first sergeant and find out where his boss was.

"Sergeant, it appears that your commander, Major Spaulding, has a problem in relation to his farm. A Major Francis and a Sergeant Major Jameston from Guard Headquarters in Minnesota would like to talk to him. He paused and glanced at Detective Donnley. The detective, he thought, knew a lot more than what he's letting on.

"Sir, all I know is that Major Spaulding left the base last evening and was headed for a restaurant near St. Cloud. After dinner he was supposed to drive down to St. Paul for the weekend." Mullins thought for only a few seconds before continuing. "I think he might be reached at his home or, if he's not there, at Fort Snelling."

"I've tried both places with no result. I would like to think this problem, whatever it is, is just a fairy tale and that everything will work out." He glanced hopefully at the first sergeant, straining to glimpse some sign of disbelief. When no sign appeared, his hope suddenly vanished.

Glancing at Donnley, the provost marshal continued. "Detective, how's your investigation going?"

"As well as to be expected, sir." Donnley surprised himself on how fast the military training came out of him, even after years away from it.

"I'd like an update on your progress, if you don't mind." The colonel looked directly at Donnley, trying to get some kind of a hint on how far the detective had progressed.

"I will have to check with my supervisor before I could do that, sir." Donnley knew the answer but thought he would give the appearance of being cooperative.

"Well, First Sergeant and Mr. Donnley, I have to leave for a meeting with the governor and the base commander. If there is anything I can help you with, please feel free to contact me." The colonel rose and began to usher the two men out of his office. "Detective, you will attempt to get the information I requested, won't you?"

Brian Donnley reached over and took the provost marshal's hand. He smiled. "I'll do my best, colonel." He turned and left the room. Tom Mullins nodded, snapped to attention, saluted, and followed Donnley. Brunch at the NCO club came next.

CHAPTER SEVENTEEN

The Sherburne County sheriff studied the written report on the Spaulding matter and looked up at his deputy. It was nearing eleven in the morning. He would like to get home and help prepare for the family get-together. One thing remained to be done. "Bill, did you make contact with any of the next of kin?"

The answer on the part of the deputy was one the sheriff was tired of hearing. He had an apparent drowning victim, and no one had been able to contact any family member of the deceased.

"Okay, Bill. Get a hold of the provost marshal up at Ripley and see if he can get someone down here to identify the deceased. Then write up anything of interest before you leave."

"Wait a minute, John." The deputy used the sheriff's first name only when he was miffed at his brother-in-law, and this was one thing that irritated him. In his mind, he was always on the short end of the family outings. Enough was enough.

"John, you know that I always have to work extra overtime when a family party is planned. Why, last Christmas I missed dinner with the family because you had me investigating what turned out to be a teenage prank. I've had enough. Why don't you assign one of the other guys just this once?"

"Bill, you never cease to surprise me. On the one hand, you scream for overtime, and on the other hand, you don't want it." John looked up at him with that election smile on his face—the one he saved for endearing his public.

Bill shook his head. "Okay, John. But I hope I can get out of here fast." That annoying smile would be wiped off his brother-in-law's face if the people ever knew how little he thought of them.

Bill dialed the number of Camp Ripley with the hope that no one would answer. He could then say he had done his job. Unfortunately, the phone was answered by the base operator, who immediately put him through to the provost marshal.

"Sir, this is Deputy Sheriff William Johnson from Sherburne County. We have a drowning victim that we believe was on duty at Camp Ripley. We have been unable to contact his family and would like to know if someone could make a positive ID."

The second lieutenant who had answered the phone was momentarily speechless. His first official act at his first summer camp as an officer would have to be some weird happening that was completely different from any of a thousand ordinary things that could have been. *Boy,* he thought. *Flub this, and I'll be back in Corporal stripes fast.* In fact, he would forever be known as having the shortest stint as a commissioned officer in history.

"Do you have any form of ID?" The shave tail did not want to jump into this without finding out as much as he could.

"Yes, we do. We have the man's military identification card, which says the man is in the reserves and is a major." The deputy was not going to give out any more information than needed. He'd be damned if he gave his brother-in-law an excuse to climb on his back again.

"Look Deputy, we have some twenty thousand men training here this period. We have numerous army units and even, excuse the expression, an Air Guard unit. Now if you can't be more specific, I can't help you—period." The lieutenant spoke authoritatively. There was nothing but silence from the deputy for almost thirty seconds.

"Lieutenant, I'm trying to do my job. His ID is red and belongs to an officer in the Air Force. His name is Peter Spaulding, and we need someone to come down and positively ID his corpse." The deputy thought he had said too much and cut himself short. He would wait for a response before saying anything more.

"Well, Deputy, we're finally getting somewhere." The lieutenant thought for only about three seconds before continuing. "There are two units that belong to the Air Guard. I'll have to contact both units before I can pin it down. Why don't you give me your phone number, and I'll call you back in about an hour?"

The deputy sighed and gave this lieutenant his number very slowly so that there would be no mistakes. "Lieutenant, I'll expect your call in about one hour." With that last frustrated expression, the deputy hung up.

The lieutenant thought for a minute before dialing the telephone number of the officer's club. He would have to contact the provost marshal, ASAP.

Dave Brokowsky heard it before anyone else. How that occurred was as common as the snow in a Minnesota winter. The story may not have been completely correct, having been passed down from one person to another, yet the crux of it was as accurate as you could get. Peter Spaulding had drowned in a Sherburne County lake.

This deputy was upset because he had to wait for someone from Camp Ripley to come and identify the body. The news traveled through the community faster than if television had announced it. The news reached the captain during the noon lunch hour when he called his wife to let her know he might be home an hour early. The captain called up Brokowksy. Brokowsky immediately called the guard headquarters. At 1:00 p.m. the two Army guardsmen were on the way to St. Cloud. Brokowsky then called his partner's number.

Brian Donnley unpacked the car, opened a can of beer, and sat on his front stoop enjoying a perfect Saturday afternoon. The telephone began to ring just when a robin landed on the shrub directly in front of him. It rang about five times before his wife answered. What she said was blocked by the screaming of the children as they fought over the last can of pop.

"Honey,"—he looked at Helen as she came out the front door, a can of beer in her hand—"who was on the phone?"

"Dave got off early and he's on the way over. He said he's got something to tell you on the case you're working on. He wants you to go to St. Cloud with him. He'll be here in about thirty minutes, so start the steak, and we'll eat before you both leave."

The provost marshal's eyes reflected a disbelief in what he was hearing. "Lieutenant, are you sure they're talking about our Major Spaulding?"

"Yes, sir!" The lieutenant stood at attention. Directly in front of the lieutenant lay a table where the governor, the provost marshal, the base commander, and the division commanding general sat eating their lunch.

He had whispered the information to the provost marshal when he had been motioned to the table. The provost marshal excused himself from the table and walked to the front desk. Taking a pen in hand, he scribbled a note on the club's stationary and handed it to the lieutenant.

"Take this note to the 1327th and hand it over to Senior Master Sergeant Mullins. Tell him it's a direct order from me. I'll be back at headquarters in about one hour. Any questions?"

The lieutenant stood at attention when he responded. "No, sir." He saluted, did a perfect about-face, and marched out the front door.

Brian Donnley and Dave Brokowsky pulled their car into the parking lot of the County Court House at 2:30 in the afternoon. Like many towns, St. Cloud did not have a full-time morgue with its own staff. The detectives would find out the particulars of the case and, since the National Guard case dealt in misappropriation of government property, there might just be a possible tie-in.

The deputy sheriff was not happy when he saw the two suits walk through the door. It meant that something big was happening and he would definitely miss the family's annual picnic. On the bright side might be they would want to see the sheriff. He would also miss the picnic, and it would serve him right.

"What can I do for you?" The deputy popped the question before the detectives had a chance to ask.

Detective Donnley looked at the deputy and immediately formed an opinion of him. He was not too smart, a political appointee, and, probably, a relative of some local big shot.

"Deputy, we're Minneapolis detectives." Flashing his ID, he continued, "We understand that you have a drowning victim by the name of Peter Spaulding in your possession."

The deputy's eyes took on a surprise look. As the question began to permeate through his mind, his eyes digressed to a look of fear.

"How did you guys know about the drowning?" The deputy did not consider it in any way that the leak could have come from his office.

"We have our methods, Deputy." Brokowsky's statement was meant as it sounded but the deputy's face suddenly turned white.

"Deputy, would you please tell us what mortuary the body is at?" Detective Donnley's voice had become hard and uncompromising.

"Yes, sir. You'll find the body of the deceased at Schmitt Funeral Home. It's located about two blocks north." The deputy decided he would be glad to have these two out of his domain as soon as possible. "If you'd like, I'll gladly call and let them know you're coming."

"That would be nice of you, Deputy. Why don't you do that?" Donnley stopped as he began to leave. "Deputy, we'll be back in about one hour. I would appreciate it if you could get the sheriff here so that we can inquire as to how the investigation is going."

"Yes, sir!" The response came with the biggest grin the deputy had ever given.

Senior Master Sergeant Mullins was settling down to a good book on tactics when the youngest looking second lieutenant he had ever seen walked into the orderly room.

"I'd like to see Sergeant Mullins." The lieutenant was surprised at the relaxed atmosphere of this Air Guard orderly room.

The sergeant stood and smiled a wonderful Irish grin. "I'm Sergeant Mullins."

"I have a note from the provost marshal for you." The lieutenant gave a folded paper to the sergeant.

Sergeant Mullins scanned the note quickly. He reached for the intercom and asked the supply sergeant to come to the orderly room immediately. "Tell the colonel. Thank you. I'll take care of the problem immediately." He closed the door and proceeded to telephone the various section chiefs who were still present for duty. Except for the tower chief, the section chiefs or their assistants were present in the orderly room within fifteen minutes.

"Gentlemen, I have just received an order from the provost marshal to proceed to the Schmitt Funeral Home in St. Cloud to make a positive ID on a drowning victim." He paused now and waited.

"I will leave here in approximately ten minutes to identify the victim. By order of the provost marshal, I am not at liberty to tell you just who the sheriff of the county thinks it is." He turned to the supply sergeant. "Mike will be in charge of the unit in my absence. Are there any questions?"

The first sergeant waited patiently for approximately one minute. "Since there are no questions, you may return to your duties. And thank you, gentlemen. I'm sure you will all do a good job in my absence." Sergeant Mullins drove out the main gate at 2:20 p.m. for a one-hour drive to St. Cloud.

CHAPTER EIGHTEEN

The sheriff was not a happy camper. His brother-in-law had the nerve to call him at the family picnic and inform him that the Spaulding case was not anywhere near being closed. Furthermore, he had informed him that two detectives from the cities wanted to talk to him. What was going on was simply not allowed in his bailiwick. It was a time that his brother-in-law found out just who god was in this county.

The sheriff looked up at the closed double doors of the old dining room of his parents' home. He had paid to have air conditioning installed in that very home just last year. It cost him dearly because of the insulation that had to be installed. They built these old 1880 farmhouses strong but, for Minnesota, the insulation was not anywhere near sufficient. *After all,* he thought, *they had used only newspaper.*

He turned toward the windows and waved at his wife, who was talking to her father's neighbor. Although there were over a hundred people at the picnic, very little noise penetrated into the house. He turned back and reached for the phone. It was time to put some pressure on that old man. Just maybe he could speed the process up and be back for the big feed.

Old Doc Thomas was sixty-nine years old and the terror of the political powers in the county. He had held the position of county coroner for almost forty years. He often criticized the investigating powers and had actively campaigned for the present sheriff's opposition. The only reason he held the job was that no one else was interested.

In about one hour he was going to perform an autopsy on Peter Spaulding. From what he understood, it would be an open-and-shut case. The victim had apparently drowned. That from that young deputy sheriff, the brother-in-law of the con-artist sheriff, set him back a bit. What have detectives from the twin cities have to do with this victim? Granted, the victim was an officer in the Air Guard. Granted, it may interest any government agency since he may or may not have been on active duty at the time of his death. But why the detectives from the twin cities?

The doctor opened his black bag and inspected the interior. Everything appeared to be in place. He snapped it shut and opened his office door. Just then the phone rang. *I hope this isn't that three-time divorcee complaining about some imaginary pain,* he thought as he reached his desk. His hand stopped just above the phone. *No,* he thought. *Not this time.* He let the phone ring as he closed the door behind him and locked up his office.

The Schmitt Funeral Home sat some 200 feet off the street on a small hill. The drive going up to the front of the mortuary curved up the hill, passed under a portico, and preceded back to the street. Halfway up the drive there was an entrance to a large parking lot that sat between the road and the base of the hill. Detective Donnley pulled the unmarked police car into the mortuary parking lot. Detective Brokowsky opened his door and strolled up the front door. The door was securely fastened. He returned to the gray Ford and slid into the passenger seat. He immediately relaxed. The two detectives would wait for the arrival of a second car.

The wait was no more than ten minutes when an old, black 1937 Chevrolet, in mint condition, pulled into the parking lot and neatly pulled up next to the gray Ford. Doc Thomas loved driving his restored jewel although, one must admit, it drove like a truck.

Doc Thomas stepped out of his rebuilt Chevy and knocked on the top of the gray car. "Hey, in there. If you're the detectives from the cities, let's get a move on."

Although Detectives Donnley and Brokowsky were taken by surprise at the loud noise on the top of their car, the two men dutifully followed the doctor up the five short steps to the shelter of the portico. "Gentlemen, we may as well wait here for Frank."

The two detectives looked at each other with surprise. "We thought you wanted us to come inside." Detective Donnley was the first of the two to voice a minor complaint.

"No. I just thought we could all wait right here. Frank will be here soon to open up." He looked expectantly at the two detectives.

Detective Donnley glanced around for the first time. The building they were standing in front of was all white with four columns holding up the protection roof of the portico. On either side of where they were standing, a blacktop driveway curved up a slight incline to pass under the rather large protecting portico. They were standing directly in front of double doors that served as the main entrance. The whole design of the building gave one the impression of Southern opulence.

Donnley looked at the doctor and, smiling broadly, held out his hand. "Doctor, I'm Detective Donnley, and my impatient friend"—he turned toward his partner—"is Detective Brokowsky."

"Yes. I was told that you would be here. What's the interest in the deceased?"

"We need to know just what Spaulding died from. If it was a drowning, okay, but we must be sure, and we would like to know if there was anything that kind of…helped the drowning along." He watched the doctor's eyes for any kind of reaction. Donnley made a mental note not to play poker with the old man.

The rattle of the old pickup truck made the three of them forget their conversation and look toward the parking lot. Next to the previous vehicles, the pickup was outclassed in every way. Its body appeared to be painted a rust and blue two-tone. The rear bumper moved up and down as the vehicle traveled from place to place. The doors were ill-fitting and the passenger side reflected a previous mishap with another vehicle. This excuse for a transportation mode carried one person. A tall, slim man dressed in freshly starched and pressed military fatigues emerged from the driver's side. Senior Master Sergeant Thomas J. Mullins had arrived at the mortuary.

He walked slowly toward the portico, obviously taking in the complete scene. As he approached the three men, he looked directly at the doctor and introduced himself as he offered him his hand.

Doc Thomas shook the sergeant's hand and marveled at the firm grip. He introduced the detectives and noticed the sergeant's eyes did not waiver.

"Sergeant, are you the person they sent from Ripley to ID the body?" Doc Thomas was blunt in his usual way.

"Yes, sir," came a quick reply.

"I believe you wanted to talk to my commander. Is that right?"

"Yes, Sergeant. A friend of yours suggested I look you up when we got to Ripley."

Just then, the door to the mortuary came open. Unlocked from the inside, the doors opening surprised the four men standing under the portico. Standing at the open entrance was a tall man of about seventy years old.

"Frank, how'd you get in without us seeing you?" Doc Thomas was the first to ask.

"Walked in through the back way, dummy." Frank's statement was accompanied by the largest grin anyone had ever seen. His blue eyes flickered with a warm friendship as he returned the doctor's gaze.

"Let me introduce you to these fine young men. Frank Schmitt, these are Detectives Donnley and Brokowsky from the cities, and this lone serviceman is Senior Master Sergeant Mullins. Frank is the owner of this establishment."

Frank took each hand as it was offered and shook it with as firm a grip as the first sergeant.

"Gentlemen, allow me to usher you into my establishment. I will leave you all in the family sitting room until the doctor and I complete our work. But first, we must await the arrival of our esteemed sheriff."

"Frank," Doc Thomas spoke first, "how about some of your famous coffee?"

The grandfather clock in the entrance sprang to life and chimed five times. The clock ceased its musical entertainment just as the sheriff entered the building.

"It's about time you showed up." Once again, Doc Thomas was the first to speak. The doctor stood and began to walk briskly toward the stairs to the lower level.

"Doc, don't be so upsetting." The sheriff's smile was wide and sincere.

Surveying the group, the sheriff turned toward the uniformed visitor. "You must be the one that Camp Ripley sent down to identify the victim." The sheriff reached out his hand.

"Yes, sir. I'm Tom Mullins, the first sergeant of the victims unit. May I see the body?" Mullins had been waiting for close to an hour and a half.

The sheriff merely nodded and motioned Mullins to follow him. "Why don't you two suits just have another cup of coffee, and we'll get this job done first." Once again, the sheriff's disarming smile stopped any retort.

Left alone, Donnley and Brokowsky began to go over their impressions of this hick sheriff and the cast of characters that were beginning to gather.

The lower level of the funeral home was dedicated to the tools of the trade. The room where the autopsy would be performed was painted in white. Frank Schmitt rolled the body from its cool interment. Pulling down the sheet, he exposed the head and the shoulders of the deceased.

Sergeant Mullins's only expression was an audible "Oh," followed by a sign of the cross.

"Well, Sergeant, is that Peter Spaulding?"

Sergeant Mullins looked up from the body and, looking directly at the sheriff, made a remark that would resound through the entire case. "Yes, sir. That's Major Spaulding. But before you continue, I must say that it is a surprise. I've served with Major Spaulding for ten years, and he was an excellent swimmer—drunk or sober. He worked out at the YMCA pool every day and entered many events. I don't think he drowned on his own. So, Doctor,"—his eyes locked on the eyes of Thomas—"I would look for something other than normal."

Doc Thomas's appearance took on the serious expression of an individual who believed everything that was being told him. Suddenly he turned to the sheriff.

"How much do you have on this supposed accident, Sheriff?"

The sheriff let out a groan. "To be honest, I don't have much. A few statements from a customer or two, which don't add up to a hill of beans. The only two that collaborate each other's testimony is the bartender and the waitress, and that's not much."

"Sheriff, may I make a suggestion?"

"Doc, I've known you for twenty years, and my objection to your suggestions never stopped you before. So go ahead."

"Let's hold up on the autopsy till tomorrow afternoon. In the meantime, you and the detectives go upstairs, get together, and put two and two together." He paused only a second before adding, "And I would include the first sergeant in this round table."

"Look Doc, you don't know what you're asking. This is my jurisdiction and my case, and I will be damned if I let the detectives, you, or the first sergeant here tell me how to run an investigation. Now I want the autopsy done today, and I think you will find it's a pure and simple drowning. Let's get on with it now."

"Okay, Sheriff. In all those twenty years, you have never taken any of my suggestions. Since the body is now in my jurisdiction, I'm taking a twenty-four-hour break and going upstairs for a cup of coffee. In the meantime, why don't you talk some shop with these detectives?"

John Clements kicked off his shoes and leaned back in his recliner. It had been a very busy Saturday. He looked over at his longtime friend and smiled. The old sarge was still as full of enthusiasm as ever. His mind was sharper than ninety-nine percent of the people he worked with. *Yes,* he thought, *Sergeant Major Emmett Massey is one hell of a man.*

The ringing of the phone interrupted his thoughts.

"Clements!" The short response to the ringing black beast was enough to let anyone who called know that it was either a proper number or a mistake of the kind that always seemed to occur at the most inappropriate time.

"Mr. Clements, this is Senior Master Sergeant Mullins. Is Sergeant Major Massey there?"

"Just a minute. Emmett, the phone is for you. It's from Mullins!"

"Sergeant Mullins ... What's the problem?"

"Emmett, Major Spaulding drowned last night in a lake near St. Cloud. We just finished the autopsy, and the doctor thinks it was murder because he was such a superb swimmer. To confirm his suspicions, he's ordered up a full test on the blood and some tissue. His lab hasn't got the equipment, so he's going to check with the state. I told him I would get a hold of you and see if your friend could get the FBI lab to process the tests."

"John, could the FBI do some blood and tissue tests for a doctor in Minnesota?"

"Sarge, is it on the Spaulding case?"

"Yes, it is."

"Tell him yes, but they should send the testing items to us ASAP."

"He said you will have it within the next twenty-four hours. He will let you know what time it will arrive. It will be on the next plane out of Minneapolis."

Massey hung up the phone and turned to John Clements. "You know, John, this thing looks bigger than just the disappearance of some military equipment or possible misuse of funds. I don't like this whole setup. It smells of a cover-up of immense proportions."

CHAPTER NINETEEN

Sergeant Major Emmett Massey looked out at the Lincoln Memorial as John Clements maneuvered his car through the slowly moving traffic, turning right on 23rd Street. *Four score and seven years ago our fathers brought forth upon this continent and new nation, conceived in liberty. and dedicated to the proposition that all men are created equal. It's funny,* thought Emmett, *how things you learn in grade school stay with you all your life.*

"John, do you think the general is going to help us?" Massey asked the question out loud without thinking and was not really expecting an answer.

"Maybe. You know I can't believe it took me two days to locate him. It's as though he just dropped off the face of the earth." John Clements was worried about just what the general could tell him. He'd been retired for almost three years and he left, as far as his friend at the Pentagon said, under kind of a cloud.

Although the route he took to the general's home was not the most direct, it provided Emmett and himself time to talk about just how they would handle a very delicate situation. He entered the Washington traffic circle and turned right again on New Hampshire. Reaching Dupont Circle, he once again blended with traffic exiting Massachusetts Avenue and joined the traffic proceeding toward the Washington Cathedral. As usual, Massachusetts Avenue was crowded with traffic going in both directions.

"Emmett, take a look to our left. That's the Navy observatory." John paused for just a second as he mentally took his position. "The general's house is on 35th Street, just south of the cathedral."

The house stood well back from the street, shaded by mature trees that kept the sun of the day at bay. Well maintained, it appeared to have been built in the 1920s and had a timeless quality that spoke of old wealth used in a subtle way.

John pulled into the driveway and stopped next to the porch. They sat for a second or two before John uttered a word. "Emmett, I know he's your friend, but let me ask the questions, please."

Emmett, for his part, simply grunted and made no verbal commitment.

They opened the screen door and stepped onto the porch. Just then, the front door opened and the general, dressed in his robe, rushed out and gave the sergeant major a bear hug. Although the general was not a big man, standing at five foot seven at the most, there was no question about his strength as he handled Emmett as though he was a feather.

"Emmett, how are you?"

"Great, sir...until last weekend."

The general's eyes and face showed his concern for his old comrade in arms. "Well, let's go in, and you can tell me about it." He held the door open as the two men passed into the entrance hall.

Seated on the sofa in the living room, the two men faced the general, who took his seat in what appeared to be his favorite rocker. Emmett began the conversation by relating his experiences over the past week. The general sat quietly until the sergeant major had finished his tale.

"What you have related to me is a serious situation. How can I help, Sergeant?"

It was then that John took over the conversation.

"General, it is Emmett's and my understanding that during the last few years of your career, you were involved with the CIA. We do not want you to compromise yourself or your family, but we thought with your connections, you could possibly find out just what is going on in Minnesota."

The general smiled at the two men and suddenly got to his feet. "Gentlemen, let me excuse myself for just a few minutes. I am going to retrieve a report I did about four years ago on a problem I ran up against in Vietnam. After you read the report, and it is classified, we can discuss what I know is happening around the country."

"General, if it is classified information, we shouldn't see it."

John's words had no sooner left his mouth when the general interrupted.

"Mr. Clements, you and Emmett here have a problem. I also have a problem. By allowing me to show you what I have, we will all, I believe, share the problem. Only you two aren't sworn to secrecy—but I am."

"Wait a minute, General." The sergeant major's voice took on the tone of command. "John here holds a top secret clearance and my clearance is no longer in effect since I pensioned off."

"How does it affect our problem?" John Clement could not understand how a report done on Vietnam four years before would have any affect on the case.

"Just read the report, and I think you'll see how it ties in." With that, the general strolled from the room.

Detective Brian Donnley greeted the patrolman at the side entrance to the Minneapolis City Hall. He moved quickly down the stairway and entered the police department. In his arms he carried a large cardboard box—one big enough to hold two standard file drawers full of records.

For the next four hours, the detective studied the files. The theft of government equipment had started approximately ten years before. The requisitioned equipment was picked up by Frank Valencio in an Air National Guard semi truck and was then moved to the base. From there, no record was available as to the disposal of the equipment. The equipment had just disappeared into the wild blue yonder.

Brian suddenly stood and stretched his lanky frame. "I think," he spoke out loud to no one in particular, "I will check with the two guardsmen and maybe take them to lunch."

Emmett laid aside the generals report and stared at both his friends. "General, you wrote this report, and what you're telling us is that the drug trade from the golden triangle is alive and well, plus it is being supported by members of the Central Intelligence Agency of the United States of America."

"That's right, Sergeant Major."

John Clements sat there in a trancelike state, shaking his head back and forth. He thought about what he and Emmett had just read and realized that the drug connection was the only thing that made sense in relation to the murders.

"General," John spoke up, "according to this report, the CIA, in order to get the cooperation of the tribes in the golden triangle, flew heroin to Macao and Taiwan by a CIA-controlled aircraft. There it was unloaded and put aboard CIA-controlled ships.

From there it was shipped to various ports in the United States, with most of it going to San Francisco."

"That's correct, Mr. Clements."

"If this report is true, why didn't the higher-ups act on it?"

"Look, the top echelons think they're winning this war. Parts of their winning combination are the so-called friendly tribes in the golden triangle. The big shots think that if we get their support, we'll be able to stop the flow of supplies into South Vietnam from North Vietnam. To do that, we help them distribute their poison. To say it again, the political forces in this town are convinced that they can win in Vietnam. They are further convinced that without the help of those tribes, they could lose. So when I turned the report in to my bosses, they went ballistic."

"What do you mean, 'went ballistic'?" Sergeant Major Massey's face was starting to turn beat red.

"They did not want to hear anything bad about their war. They refused to believe that our allies in this campaign were more concerned with making huge amounts of money than with defeating our enemy." The general paused now and took a deep breath. "Add that to some agents, officers, and senior NCOs who are more than willing to cut themselves in on the gravy train, and you have a situation which grows rapidly out of control and is disastrous for the future wellbeing of the nation."

The two visitors sat in silence for a good five minutes until the general broke the ice. "You may keep a copy of that report; I have the original." His wink and slight nod gave a warning.

"But General, if this gets out, they will crucify you." Clements was the first to respond.

"It's too late for that. My wife died two years ago, and I have no children. As far as I'm concerned, my time on earth is limited in any case. No . . . the report gets mailed to a friend of mine tomorrow morning."

"If this is picked up by any reputable newspaper, you will be a hero to the anti-war effort and a traitor to many of your friends. It's not a good way to end a fine career." Emmett Massey knew that when the establishment got through with the general, he would be a broken man.

"General, if you need anything at all, I mean *anything*, you call me. Why, you might even like to stay at my out-of-the-way cabin and fish every day."

"Sergeant, I might take you up on that." The general smiled, shook their hands, and ushered them to the front door. "Oh, before you leave, Sergeant, I have some pictures you might like to have; most of them are with you and me in our long careers. Just wait on the porch, and I'll be right back."

It was all of five minutes before the general returned with a box wrapped in brown paper. "You'll find that the pictures are very interesting."

"Thank you, sir." Sergeant Major Emmett Massy snapped to attention and saluted his old comrade in arms.

The general, surprised, returned the salute and then reached out and hugged the sergeant in a warm embrace. The slight hint of a tear began to roll down his check.

"General,"—Clements suddenly expressed a concern—"what about the four other men who signed on that report?"

The expression that came over the general's face said more than any mere words could express. He looked around as though trying to see if they were being spied on before speaking.

"Don't worry about them; the colonel was killed in a one car accident on US 1 near Fairfax Station, Virginia. The major got killed in the Vietnam war. One of the lieutenant colonels is in the field with an infantry unit in Nam." The general paused. "I think he's a marked man, and the fourth one is a prisoner of war in North Vietnam."

"Gentlemen, I think it's time for me to meet a friend of mine. Nice meeting you, Mr. Clements. Sergeant Massey, be careful out there and take good care of yourself." He patted the sergeant's arm, closed the door, turned, and left the porch.

'Clements looked at his watch. "Sergeant, you have a plane to catch. Let's get a move on."

CHAPTER TWENTY

The National Guard C-130 lifted from the runway at Andrews Air Force Base some ten minutes late. Opposite a pallet of electronics gear sat the lone passenger, retired Sergeant Major Emmett Massey. He thought about opening the box that the general had given him. No, he would leave the box as it was until he arrived safe in Minneapolis.

A movement behind the pallet that lay directly in front of him attracted his attention. The appearance of the crew chief surprised him. Emmett looked up and smiled as the master sergeant came up to him. "Sarge, would you like a cup of coffee?"

"That would hit the spot. How was your stay in Washington?"

"Pretty good, except I had to go to work about four this morning."

"Getting the plane ready for departure?"

"No. We were loaded last night. It seems there was a problem with the electronics. Got it fixed about eight this morning. By the time I got cleaned up and ate breakfast, it was too late to catch up on my sleep."

"What was wrong?" Emmett, always interested in electronics, dreamed of having a ham station.

"Oh, apparently there was a short in the electrical circuits. One of the ground crew tried to fix it and just made it worse. I got called by an NCO friend of mine who had come across the airman about 3:30 in the morning."

"Lucky for us your NCO friend came along. Did he know the airman?"

"That's the funny thing—this airman was assigned to the unit just three days ago. Seems he came highly recommended by his last unit. In any case, he was performing a routine check on the radio when the short occurred. Why do you ask?"

"No reason. It just seems kind of odd that this airman, who is new in this unit, would have a problem like that occur." The sergeant major fell quiet as he let his last words hang as though expecting an answer.

"You know, Sarge, that does sound kind of strange. In fact, a radio check is rare at that time of morning unless it's asked for." He looked at Emmett with a worried look in his eyes. "I think I'll check with the major and see if anyone in the cockpit asked for a check on our radios."

Within five minutes the crew chief reappeared with a worried look on his face. Emmett's suspicions were right.

"No one in the cockpit asked to have the radios checked last night. So the airman had no business in our aircraft." He looked at Emmett. "The major told me to check all electrical circuits and any other things that may come to mind. Quite frankly, I'm worried." He turned away and began to make his way to the front of the aircraft. "Oh, Sarge, you better put your chute on."

"Right." Emmett's answer, though short, sounded as worried as the crew chief's look.

Emmett looked down at his bag. The pictures must be saved if anything happens to the aircraft. His instincts told him that the general had given him more than just pictures. He had not opened the box, but he felt that it bore directly on the motive for all the killings.

The words from the flight chief woke him from his thoughts. "We have a fire warning light on the right outboard engine. We've cut the engine and we're diverting to Volk Field." The sergeant shook his head and walked back to his station.

Frank Valencio sat on the screened porch of the cabin and looked out at the lake as the sun began to set in the western sky. It had been a little over a week since this craziness all began. Two of his close friends were dead. It was hard to believe that these senseless killings were over a few stolen items. His friend, Sergeant Major Massey, should have been here. Where he could be was anyone's guess.

Massey's friends, the owners of Frank's latest hideaway, were extremely upset by his lateness. They had been assured that he would return by late afternoon. As the hours passed, turning the bright beauty of the day toward the dark of a moonless night, the senior couple began to worry more openly.

Frank checked his pistol, a .45 caliber automatic, and put it back in its hiding place. He hoped he would never use it. He leaned back on the couch with his eyes staring into the slowly darkening night sky. The couple had finally gone to bed. He let his mind go back to the night, or rather early morning, of his escape. He could even hear their voices as they asked questions that meant nothing to him. He hoped his wife and daughter were safe.

Frank looked to his right, toward a sound of voices that could be heard in the distance. He liked this porch. Its wraparound construction allowed one to view the lake to the front of the cabin. The second view was from the corner of the porch and allowed one an excellent site for watching the road leading up from the county highway some 600 yards to the east. The couch was placed so that while it faced the south side where the side door allowed entrance into the cabin, it also allowed you a view of the lake and the front entrance. It was an ideal place to rest and still cover both approaches. He closed his eyes and allowed his mind to concentrate on the sounds around him.

Tom Hanson swore under his breath. "I slipped, and the door got away from me." He looked sheepishly at his partner.

Snell answered, showing his displeasure. "Yeah. That and a nickel will put us both in hell."

It had been more than a week before they tracked Valencio down to this cabin in the woods. Hopefully there would be only two present. The word was that the retired sergeant major who owned this getaway was one tough old bird. Well, the word was out to eliminate both of them.

They had approached the darkened cabin from the woods. No sound could be heard from within. While Hanson held the screen door, Snell took almost thirty seconds to pick the simple lock. He pushed the side door open slowly and allowed Hanson to take up his position at the front entrance.

Once positioned, he waited for his partner to pick the lock on the front door. His thinking was not on the killing that was about to begin but on the silence of the night. It was as though the whole of creation waited for a final crescendo.

It seemed like forever before Hanson heard his partner's booming voice. He moved through the door and flashed his light around the inside of the cabin. *My God,* he thought, *the place is empty.* He could hear Snell in what appeared to be the kitchen, screaming at the top of his lungs.

"The whole place is empty! What are we supposed to do now?" The question was more like a shout to the heavens than a question to be answered. Snell kicked over a table, picked up a chair, and threw it at the refrigerator. Suddenly he turned and looked with disgust as his partner approached from the front door.

Hanson surveyed the scene and smiled. "You sure know how to announce our presence."

He bent over, picked up the chair, and quietly put it back where it came from. He turned the table right side up and hoped the scratch on its top had been there before. The slight dent in the door of the refrigerator might not be noticed. Once again, he surveyed the scene and moved to the telephone and the table that served as a desk next to the wall.

He spotted a marker on a page and, turning to that page, found onc address and telephone number circled. The address indicated a small village not more than five miles from where they were. Hanson smiled to himself. *The old sarge was not that sharp,* he thought.

"Snell, it's ten o'clock. We'll look around here for a while and then we'll head south for about five miles. I think we'll get our men by midnight."

Emmett Massey thanked the colonel for the ride in from Volk Field, Wisconsin. The C-130 had touched down at 1600 with all the base fire engines in attendance. There had been no damage, and the crew, their one passenger, and the cargo were safe on the ground with no harm. Within a half hour, he had connected with the colonel, flying himself back to Minneapolis in his own Cessna.

Yet even with such luck, it took him till 2000 before he arrived at Snelling. In about two hours, he would be at his friend's home. He crossed the parking lot and unlocked his pickup truck. He placed his bag and the box that the general had given him on the passenger side. Sliding into the driver's seat, he reached into his bag and removed the.45 pistol. He wondered how Frank was doing and hoped he had taken good care of this pistol's mate. He looked at his watch—2015—time to get going. He started the truck, shifted the engine into first gear, and began his drive north.

CHAPTER TWENTY-ONE

Twenty-three twenty-five—a new personal record for driving from Fort Snelling to this small town just five miles from the cabin. Not bad, Massey thought, as he swung into the driveway of the town's only gas station. He pulled the car up to the pumps and stepped from his truck. He would call his friends from here and maybe pick Frank up, and then they could stay at his place for the night.

"Hi, Sergeant Major." The owner of the gas station had come in to make up his deposit for the next morning and to close the station at midnight.

"Hi, Bud." The sergeant major fumbled with his keys.

"Say, are you headed out to the Robinson place?"

"Sure am, Bud. Why did you ask?"

"Some men were asking for the Robinson's place about five minutes ago."

Massey's face turned into an expression that could only be called a mixture of fear and anger. "What men?" was his only comment, but it was made in such a way that even the most hardened individual would have answered immediately.

"There were two of them, Sarge. What's the problem?"

"How long ago did they leave?"

"Not more than five minutes ago." Bud was beginning to have fearful feelings.

Massey nodded his head and turned to leave. "Call the sheriff and get them out to the Robinson's place ASAP."

Bud turned to hurry to his office while Massey returned to his vehicle and retrieved his .45 pistol from the front seat.

He started his truck and deftly shifted it into gear. Screeching in all three gears, he raced down the main street, heading toward his friend's cabin.

Snell and Hanson pulled their car up slowly to the access road with its lights turned off. The two men parked the car close to the driveway and began a long, slow movement toward the cabin some 300 yards away. They could not see a thing, and movement through the thick underbrush along the gravel drive was tedious and purposely slow.

Glancing at the illuminated hands of his watch, Snell could see the large hand slowly approaching midnight. Both men drew their guns and readied themselves for the last fifty yards.

Frank Valencio lay on his couch listening for the sounds. He had lain awake for about one hour and felt as though something was going to happen.

His hand slid around the.45, and he pulled it out from its hiding place. He glanced directly above his position and thought about reaching for the yard light. No, he thought. He would wait until he was sure. He leaned back and waited for some sound. That was it; the crickets were silent and the birds had quieted down. Someone was approaching the cabin.

Snell heard the crash of the hood from his position just fifty feet from the cabin. He looked to his rear with a sudden fear reflected in his spine. He looked again at where the car was parked but could not see anything.

Hanson heard the same sound, but from his position in front of the cabin, he could not tell where the sound came from. He stopped for just a few seconds and began to move toward the front door of the cabin.

Frank Valencio heard the sound and suddenly realized that it was meant as a warning. He reached up and switched on the light just as Tom Hanson was ten steps from the front door.

Hanson reacted by raising his hand with his pistol toward his eyes. The blinding light had caught him unaware. Valencio aimed and pulled the trigger. The boom of the.45 sounded like a cannon as it echoed through the woods. Tom Hanson fell backward and crashed to the ground with a bullet in his right shoulder.

Snell heard the shot and immediately moved toward the side door. He was blinded by the strong light and knew he had to get away from the whiteness that had suddenly surrounded him. Frank spotted the figure some twenty-five feet away and quickly fired a round in that direction.

Snell swore under his breath as the bullet came within an inch of his ear. *That guy is good,* was his last thought, as he sprawled next to the cabin. Whoever was firing would have to come out of the cabin to see him. He would have a clear shot, and then it would be his turn to become the hunter.

Hanson lay there in front of the cabin not moving. The kick of the slug had torn into him, making a mess of his shoulder, and had thrown him to the ground. Suddenly he saw a truck roar out the darkened path. *Snell's in trouble now,* he thought as he tried to rise, only to fall back. With that thought, he lost consciousness.

Snell also saw the truck as it moved quickly toward the side of the cabin. He rolled to his right, ending with his back to the logs of the cabin and his front looking toward the oncoming pickup. He raised his pistol, and suddenly the truck braked to a halt just at the edge of the lighted area. A figure rolled out of the driver's side and quickly sprawled on the ground.

He moved his pistol toward the sprawling figure only to see it disappear into the darkness of the woods. He fired his.9 mm once and hoped the shot would do some damage.

Massey could see the intruder lying next to the log cabin and took careful aim at the figure. The wood above the figure splintered as the shot missed the head by not more than three inches. They had the intruder caught between Frank and himself with light showing in all directions from the cabin and headlights of the still-running pickup truck.

Massey shouted out in hopes of getting a response. "Frank, you okay?" A shot hitting slightly above his head came from the figure now attempting to make his silhouette as small as possible.

The Robinsons woke at the first shot, and within a second, Jimmy Robinson pushed his wife to the floor. He rolled out of the bed and made for the front room, his shotgun in hand.

Once again Massey began to take careful aim, when the voice of Jimmy Robinson came booming out of the cabin. "We're fine, Emmett, and I've got my shotgun, just in case,"

Just then, Massey began to respond as a siren broke into the exchange. The sheriff's car came racing up the driveway, braking just short of hitting the rear of Massey's pickup.

In just that second, Snell began to move toward the rear of the cabin, the darkness suddenly swallowing up his receding form. Massey, momentarily distracted by the sheriff's noisy arrival, turned back, only to find that the intruder was no longer in sight.

Massey yelled at the sheriff, "John, follow me. He's trying to make a break for it."

Sheriff John Miller, a thirty-year veteran, moved toward the sound of Massey's voice and waved his deputy toward the road and the disabled car they had pinpointed as they approached the driveway.

Snell knew he was in trouble. He had to work his way back to the car and hope that he could escape before that sergeant major and the sheriff kept him from reaching it.

Just then, Snell broke out into the open on the access road some seventy-five feet from his car. He sprinted the last few feet, opened the door,and slipped inside, hoping that he still had time to escape. He turned the key and nothing happened. He turned it again...still nothing. He tried to think. *Heck, the whole operation is falling apart.* He opened the door, cracked the hood, and began to slip out of the driver's side.

"Hold it right there." The words spoken by the deputy surprised Snell. He stood there just for a few seconds as he attempted to judge the situation.

The movement of his right hand was so fast that, to the deputy, it seemed like a blur. With one motion, Snell turned as he dropped to the ground, bringing his.9 mm into position for firing. The bullet flew through the air, hitting the deputy in his left leg. The deputy dropped to the ground and fired one round toward the now-rolling figure of Snell.

Snell moved quickly through the tall grass between the county road and the access road.

Meanwhile, Massey and the sheriff were closing in on their prey. Massey suddenly loomed up directly in front of the errant Snell, who turned only to see the sheriff standing over him with a.38 Smith and Wesson pointing directly at his head. With that, Snell allowed his gun to drop from his hand and rolled over on his back.

The ambulance pulled off with the deputy and a seriously wounded Hanson on board. A second deputy's car pulled off with their prisoner and would be back at the county jail within the next fifteen minutes.

The Robinsons, the sheriff, and Massey sat facing Frank Valencio. The identification cards of both prisoners sat on the coffee table in front of the sheriff. The major question was why they were snooping around a private residence at midnight. Once that was answered, a second question had to be answered. Just why was this organization operating within the United States?

Massey was the first to speak. "Sheriff, I think it's time for Frank, you, and I to have a private discussion on just what is occurring. I would suggest we move this discussion over to your office, okay?"

Jimmy Robinson just looked at both of them with a "drop dead" expression on his face. His wife and he had just gone through a very exciting period in their long life together, and he'd be damned if they cut him out of the explanation. "No, way." Jimmy was smiling broadly now. "Sheila and I want to know the whole sordid mess."

Massey smiled and excused himself. "I need to move my truck," was his only comment.

The sheriff watched him go out the side entrance to the porch and turned to Jimmy. "Jimmy, we all have been longtime friends. I think the sergeant major is right. It's time to leave."

Jimmy's expression told it all; he was disappointed. He felt that he was being excluded from very important and exciting information.

"Sheila, talk some sense into your husband. Thanks for your hospitality." With that, the sheriff handed Frank his crutches, helped him stand, and reached out to hold the door.

It was then that Frank asked to see the IDs of the intruders. The sheriff thought for just one moment. "Mr. Valencio, go ahead." And he handed them over.

Frank stood leaning against his crutches and studied the pictures for a minute. He shook his head, and his face grew grim.

"Sheriff, the guy named Snell is the one who shoved my buddy out of the helicopter door. He killed him."

The Robinsons looked at the sheriff and realized the gravity of the situation.

The sheriff looked at Frank. "What are you talking about?"

"I'll explain it to you when Massey and I get to your office, okay?"

"I guess so, since I have a feeling everyone knows more about what's going on than I do." With that, the sheriff held the door open as Frank hobbled down the steps of the cabin.

Frank maneuvered himself into the truck bed of Massey's pickup, turned, and smiled at the Robinsons. Waving, he shouted out, "Hey Sarge, I'm ready back here, but take it easy on the dirt roads." The truck and the sheriff's car slowly pulled away. The time was 3:00 a.m.

CHAPTER TWENTY-TWO

The sheriff's office looked as though it was right out of the 1890s. Even the jail cells appeared to have been unchanged since the early part of the century. The front entrance led directly into the office that had two oak desks with one revolving oak chair, and the only nod to the latter part of the century was a padded executive chair at the sheriff's desk.

It was as though Mayberry RFD had been moved lock, stock, and barrel, to the middle of eastern Minnesota and planked down in the middle of nowhere. The jail cells were in a different part of the building, which was reached from the main office through a door directly across from the front door.

The three men in question—actually four, if you included the prisoner in the number-four jail cell—had been in a state of sleep since their arrival at 3:30 a.m. Frank lay sprawled on an overstuffed couch, dead to the world. Massey was asleep in an overstuffed chair that had been drafted into use as a side chair after it had served five years in the sheriff's home.

The sheriff had checked the jail cell when he arrived just to make sure that the jail's only prisoner was comfortable. He had completed some paperwork by four in the morning and had leaned back in his executive chair and promptly went to sleep.

The grandfather clock, which stood next to the entrance of the jail cells, chimed eight when the front door suddenly swung open. The chimes were then joined by the squeaking hinges which, in turn, caused the sheriff to bolt upright.

"Tom! How many times must I tell you to be careful when you enter this building?" The sheriff did not like being disturbed from sleep, even when it was on the village's time. "Tom, keep it quiet. I don't want to wake our guests."

The sheriff had relieved Tom, his second deputy, at 3:30 and had thought he would have slept in late. It had been 12:30 when Tom had gotten the call at home. He'd rushed to the scene when he heard that Bill had been wounded. He had then roughly escorted the prisoner to jail. What he was doing here four and a half hours after being relieved was a guess that the sheriff was not awake enough to wonder about.

"Tom, what are you doing down here, anyway?"

"Sheriff, I've got a couple of questions to ask you about our prisoner. Something's bothering me, and I've got to make sure that what we're doing is okay."

"Okay, Tom. Go ahead and ask."

"The guy asked for a telephone call, and I did what you said and told him that he would have to wait till you talked to him." Tom looked squarely at the sheriff. "He said he was CIA and he would see that we all went to jail if he did not get his one telephone call."

"Tom,"—the sheriff looked at Tom—"he is CIA. He almost killed your buddy and he attacked a civilian target in my bailiwick." He paused to allow his mind to separate itself between vengeance and justice. "The CIA has a mandate from congress to operate outside the United States. In this case, they breached their mandate. I, therefore, want to check a few more items before I decide to charge him. Okay?

Tom looked at his boss and smiled. "Okay."

Of the two sleeping beauties, it was Emmett Massey that spoke up. "Sheriff, I couldn't help overhearing the conversation. I think I may have something that may bear on this case. Let me get a package from my truck, and I'll be right back."

The sheriff just waved as Emmett disappeared out the front door. He reappeared about two minutes later with a rather large package under his arm. Laying it down in the center of the sheriff's desk, he began to open the gift from his friend in Washington.

Brian Donnley looked at his partner long and hard. The information he had come up with was so improbable that it flew in the face of his intelligence. That the government was sneaking drugs into the United States was almost laughable. The tale had to be a huge lie told by the anti-Vietnam crowd in order to discredit the whole war effort. The lie probably was started somewhere in Hanoi or Beijing or maybe even Moscow.

Dave Brokowski laughed out loud at his partner's accusation. "No, Brian. This information comes directly from someone who would not lie under any circumstances. What you're saying then is that the United States government, in order to start a war, went into the drug trade in a big way."

"No. What I am saying is that someone who may have worked for a large government organization is involved in smuggling drugs into the United States." Dave paused for just about five seconds before he plunged on. "It is not necessarily the United States government, but some agency officials who work for the government that have decided to branch out on their own."

Brian still did not believe his ears. "Buddy, tell me where you got this information, and let me judge just how reliable it is."

"Brian, I wish I could, but there is a military law to be concerned about." He knew he had already breached the military code. "I can tell you this—the person who called me on this works in a suburb on the police department. He knows both you and I, and he is an officer in the National Guard. Now with that, you ought to be able to figure it out yourself."

"Oh, my god." Brian suddenly reacted. "You really are telling the truth. But how did our friend get a hold of you?"

"Simple, he had to take a run this morning to Minneapolis. He stopped at a restaurant to have breakfast when he decided to call me at home." Dave laughed out loud at the thought of getting awakened at 4:30 in the morning. "Now let's try to figure out how this little tidbit fits into the whole…if it does."

"Dave, we have been looking for a motive to kill our clerk. Right now, his commander does not look like the type to commit murder, nor did he know the right people, and since he's dead, we may have a double homicide on our hands."

"Besides, I'll bet that whoever it was eliminated our commander last Friday night."

Massey handed the report to the sheriff, sat back, and waited for the sheriff to page through the some thirty pages.

Reading the report, the sheriff looked up with a surprised look on his face. "The report mentioned a project called 'Phoenix,' which the CIA was running. Apparently they were executing Vietcong or people that they thought were Vietcong. It also mentioned something about drugs being brought into the States."

Frank Valencio lay quietly as he listened to the conversation. Suddenly he shouted at the sheriff, "Hey, sheriff, have you booked that guy we caught last night?"

"Not yet. Why do you ask?" The sheriff turned so he could face Frank.

"He's the guy who pushed my buddy out of that helicopter. He's the one who killed him."

Massey, remembering what Frank had told him, also looked at Frank. "Are you sure, Frank?"

"Darn right, I'm sure. He's the one."

"If that's the case, I'm going to book him for murder and attempted murder until we can verify what Frank says."

Turning back to the pictures, he pointed out a second flaw—one of the pictures showed a line of C-130s, but the back of the picture mentioned ten aircraft by number, yet only seven were shown in the pictures.

Again the sheriff looked at the pictures and began to smile. "Emmett, what the pictures don't show is what the message is about. First, there is a field with no warehouse and now a line of aircraft without all the aircraft."

The sergeant major looked at the sheriff and smiled. "You got it, buddy. The first thing we do is find out if any of these aircraft are still on the Air Force inventory. I think I'll call my friend in Washington, John Clements. If anybody can find out about these aircraft, he can."

CHAPTER TWENTY-THREE

Special Agent John Clements sat at his desk and pondered the list that Massey had called and given to him. It had taken three hours to check out the aircraft, and some had been reported destroyed in Nam. What was strange is that his friend in the Pentagon had reported that there had been a crash at Minneapolis-St. Paul International Airport of one of those aircraft. In effect, it was a ghost aircraft.

If it was connected to the CIA, it could tie into what the general had told him and Massey. More importantly, these could all be connected to a major drug running by a branch of the federal government. If so, he had better have Massey warn the two guardsmen that they should be extremely careful once they started their investigation at the crash site. Reaching for the phone, Clements dialed the State National Guard Bureau.

Major Francis got the call from John Clements just as he and Senior Master Sergeant Jameston were leaving their office in St. Paul. They should reach MSP in about thirty minutes. They would have to check with the FAA before they began their investigation at the crash site. It may be nothing. Yet again, they just might get lucky.

At the site of the accident, the FAA investigators allowed the two guardsmen to look over the wreckage. The C-130 had crashed, carrying five personnel and twelve fireproof files, which were locked with a bar going down the front of the files. The combination locks on them were all set so that in order to get into them, you would have to use a saw or file to cut them off.

The FAA investigator by the name of Jerry Haglund escorted the guardsmen around the site and stopped suddenly in front of one the files that had been damaged. "Gentlemen, we are highly interested in these files. As you can see, these file sides were peeled in the crash and where there was supposed to be a fireproofing material between the walls of the file cabinets, there appeared to be packages of drugs—heroin, we think. We have already called the DIA."

Major Francis looked seriously at Mr. Haglund. "We would like a copy of your report when it's ready." "That's fine, Major Francis. We'll let you know."

The sheriff finished fingerprinting his prisoner and booked him for murder and attempted murder, at which time, the prisoner asked for a telephone call. Unfortunately for the sheriff, it was long-distance to Washington, DC. The law firm of Baker, Bush, and Libby was well-known for its Republican connections. It was also known for its connections with the administration.

"You've got a prestigious law firm, Mister." The sheriff was surprised that such a well-known firm would handle this case without even asking what it was all about.

Just then the telephone rang. "Sheriff's office; sheriff speaking."

"Sheriff, this is Detective-Sergeant Donnley of the Minneapolis Police Department. My partner and I are working on a case in Minneapolis and the Guard is also involved. We understand that you had a problem in your area with a couple of guardsmen. Is that correct?"

"Yes. But what's this about?"

"We think the cases are connected. In fact, we think the CIA is involved, and it may be connected to drugs being brought into the States." Donnley paused, waiting for a response.

"Okay. I think your suppositions are correct. I just booked one prisoner for murder and attempted murder, and I have another one in the hospital under guard. Their attorneys are flying in from Washington, DC. They'll be here Monday morning."

Donnley thought for a while before responding. "Let me talk to my guardsmen first, and I'll get back to you."

"Well, that's fine. I'll be here for the rest of the day." With that last remark, the sheriff hung up.

Donnley called Major Francis and told him about the lawyers. He hung up the phone and looked at his sergeant. "I think we justbetter call Clements again. There's some big law firm from the capital coming in on Monday for these killers."

John Clements was having a wonderful Sunday afternoon with his family. The grill was just right for the steaks to be put on, the potatoes were almost done, and the corn was fast becoming ready to put on the plates. Just then the phone rang, and his wife picked it up to answer. The expression on her face said it all.

Without a word, he moved into his home and asked his wife to watch the meal as he took the phone out of her hand. "Clements..." He sat and listened asMajor Francis briefed him on what was transpiring.

"One of the partners in that firm is a friend of mine from law school days. I'll give him a call and see what he knows about it. If I can, I'll see if he can have his firm back off. It would be costly, and I don't think they have an office in Minnesota.

It was 6:00 p.m. on that Sunday when Clements contacted his friend. “Bill, it’s John Clements. I understand your law firm is taking on a case in Minnesota Monday morning; is that right?”

“It wouldn’t surprise me, but we don’t have an office in Minnesota. Why do you ask?”

“There have been two murders in Minnesota and possibly another. All were Air National Guard members, and the police think it has something to do with the CIA. Now this isn’t just suspicion. There is a witness to one of the killings, and there are six witnesses to attempted murders on a deputy sheriff and another guard member. In addition, there is drug smuggling involved, and the FAA has called in the DIA after a plane crashed in Minneapolis-St. Paul International Airport.” Special Agent Clements stopped now to allow the information to sink in.

After listening to Clements’s words, Bill Thomas allowed himself to think about what he has just heard. “John, I don’t know what to say.”

“Well, I think you had better have your firm back off from this case. The judge in Minnesota is getting ready to issue a search warrant on certain property, and I don’t think you want to be involved.”

“I’ll see what I can do. And thanks for giving me a heads-up on this. We didn’t know about the drugs or two of the murders. I’ll let you know tomorrow morning for sure. Okay?”

“That’s fine, old buddy.” With that, Special Agent Clements hung up and immediately called the Minnesota Guard headquarters in St. Paul.

“Sheriff, this is Detective Donnley in Minneapolis. I just got off the phone with Major Francis, and he just got word from Washington that the law firm that your prisoners called have decided not to handle your prisoners’ case. Basically, your prisoners are being hung out to dry. We’ll know tomorrow morning for sure.”

The sheriff hung up the phone and entered the hallway that separated the cells. Turning to his only prisoner, he smiled. "Young man, if you need an attorney, one can be appointed for you."

The response was immediate. "You know I've already got one, and that firm I called is the best in the nation."

"I'm sorry about that, but I was just notified that your big-shot attorneys are not coming in and are not going to represent you."

Snell's face suddenly turned white as he realized that his employers were cutting him and his partner loose, and they would soon face a judge and jury for their part in the fiasco that the press was now calling the "Guard Murders."

Detective Sergeant Donnley was relieved that the murderers were caught and would soon face trial. He looked forward to a peaceful night with his family, and possibly another ninety-six hours with no calls to homicide.